I hoisted the box of candles into my arms. "Trust me, I've handled more sophisticated gear than this."

I was walking past Marcus when my shoulder accidentally brushed against his. Before I could take another step I felt an intense pressure on my arm.

"Ow!" I dropped the box, sending the candles flying across the floor. Marcus was gripping my arm. It felt like he was trying to push his fingers all the way through my flesh. I was simply startled at first, but that feeling gave way to panic as the pain in my arm intensified.

"You have pushed back the curtain too far," Marcus said.

Only, it wasn't really Marcus. A voice was coming from his mouth, but it wasn't his voice. In fact, my first thought was that it wasn't even a *human* voice. It was something between a hiss and a whisper, neither male nor female.

It was, quite simply, otherworldly.

And not a good world.

Marcus's gaze was fixed on me, but his eyes looked strange, like the blacks of his pupils had spread and swallowed the rest of his eyeball. I tried to pull away, but his grip was cement. If he squeezed any harder, my arm would break.

My legs gave out and I sank to the floor. Marcus was still clenching my arm, but now he was slowly twisting it as he dug his fingers into my flesh. I was fairly certain that the sensation would be similar to getting shot in the arm.

"You have pushed back the curtain too far," Marcus repeated. "There is a price to be paid."

# one hundred candles

## mara purnhagen

**HARLEQUIN**®
**TEEN**

# HARLEQUIN®
# TEEN

ISBN-13: 978-0-373-21023-7

ONE HUNDRED CANDLES

Recycling programs for this product may not exist in your area.

*c*
*URN*
*AGEN*

## ACKNOWLEDGMENTS

Thank you to my wonderful editor, Tara Parsons,
and everyone at Harlequin Teen.

Special thanks to John & Martha Lohrstorfer,
Margean Gladysz, Pam Mishowski, Maureen Warren Ray,
Coleen Travers, and Cheri Warren.

As always, thanks to Robert Lettrick
for his awesome skills in technical creativity.

And no book is ever complete until I thank the home team:
Joe, Henry, Quinn, and Elias. I love you—now let me get some sleep.

For more than one hundred reasons,
this one is for Tina Dubois Wexler

# one

I would never get used to spending Christmas in an insane asylum. My parents laughed and said that, after seventeen years, I should have looked forward to it, but I would much rather sit in front of a roaring fire with a mug of hot chocolate listening to Christmas carols instead of this year's version of holiday cheer: roaming the barren hallways of an empty sanitarium in a quest for restless energy.

After opening presents in yet another beige-and-floral hotel room and wolfing down the hotel's complimentary cinnamon rolls, my family piled into our van and drove nearly an hour west of Cleveland to Lake Sanitarium, a somber-looking brick monstrosity that was, despite its name, located nowhere near a lake. Dad opened the massive front doors by shoving against them with his entire body. My teeth chattered as the five of us climbed the stairs, our footsteps echoing until we reached a large, empty room on the third floor.

"It's colder inside than it is outside," I muttered to my sister when we reached our destination.

"Welcome to Ohio," Annalise replied. "It's supposed to be nearly seventy degrees back home today."

I groaned and thought of our house in South Carolina. I could picture my best friend, Avery, taking her little dog for a warm winter walk, shading her eyes from the sunlight. Or Noah, who told me that he grilled steaks for his mom every Christmas. And Jared—well, I didn't know what Jared did for the holidays. We were friends, but he was an intensely private person, and he rarely offered details about his life.

I glanced out one of the grimy, narrow windows onto the sprawling white lawn of the sanitarium. The perfectly undisturbed snow was lovely to look at, but I was too cold to enjoy it.

"How are we doing, girls?" Dad clapped his hands together and walked over to where Annalise and I stood huddled in the corner.

"We're freezing." I could see my breath, which was the same pale color as the cinder-block walls.

"Well, the best way to stay warm is to keep moving. How about helping Shane with the equipment?"

I sighed, sending another puff of white into the air, and hurried across the empty room. There was no furniture to offer a clue of what the space had once been used for, but I guessed it had served as a massive holding area for the insane people who had lived there decades earlier. I knew the building had housed thousands of dejected people. Many of them had died here, as well, earning it the nickname Last Stop Lake.

"Hey, kid, can you give me a hand?" Shane was struggling to sort through a nest of cables and camera wires. I knelt down next to him and began picking through the different cables.

"This is a mess," I complained. Shane was usually more organized. He'd worked as my parents' full-time cameraman since I was a baby, traveling all over the world with us to produce documentaries about the paranormal. I'd never seen his equipment so scattered.

"It's a little chaotic," Shane admitted. "Been distracted lately, I guess."

I snorted. "Distracted, huh? I wonder what's causing that?"

He shot me a look but said nothing. Shane had begun dating Trisha, the mother of my friend Noah, right around Halloween. They were always together, it seemed, and while I liked seeing Shane crazy about someone, Noah was not nearly as thrilled.

"She's acting like a teenager!" he told me during AV. It was the one class we shared together, and we usually worked as a team to edit the daily school news footage. "I'm supposed to be doing this, not her."

"And anyone in particular you'd like to be immature over?" I teased him.

His eyes had widened and he immediately blushed. I suspected he harbored a little bit of a crush on a freshman girl I'd seen hanging around his locker, but he hadn't admitted to it yet, and I didn't ask a lot of questions. We had gone to homecoming together, an event I thought might lead to something more. At the end of the night, though, he'd just smiled, said he had a great time and left. That was it. I was totally confused, but Avery said that maybe Noah and I were destined to be good friends. Since I would be graduating in a few months, it didn't make a lot of sense to start something with a junior, but I had been hoping that Noah and I could be more than just "friends."

After sorting through the web of wires, I helped Shane set up a tripod, then returned to a corner of the huge room and pulled out my cell phone. Being the daughter of paranormal investigators provided a few perks. My parents were always buying different gadgets, and they appreciated great technology, so when I asked for a new cell phone for Christmas they gave me the best one they could find. While they set up their equipment to begin their research, I stood by the window and attempted to download my email.

"Hey, Charlotte. Do you have a signal yet?" Annalise walked over, gathering her long black hair into a ponytail. My sister had gorgeous wavy hair, just like our mom. I, on the other hand, inherited our dad's straight locks, which I'd recently chopped shorter, so that it was just long enough to tuck behind my ears.

"It's faint," I told Annalise.

She sat on the cement floor. "I can't believe how much I miss Mills."

I rolled my eyes. "It's only been three days."

"It feels like three years."

I'd never seen my older sister so head-over-heels for a guy. I'd met Mills two months earlier, in Charleston. Annalise was a junior at the college there and Mills was a grad student. We were in Charleston to put an end to a seriously supernatural situation, but our gathering had also served to introduce Mills to the family. Mom loved him. Dad was not as thrilled.

"He's a little old for her, isn't he?" he asked me the day after we met Mills.

"He's just a couple years older," I pointed out. "Besides, aren't you five years older than Mom?"

"That's not the point," he grumbled.

I wondered if Dad would have the same disgruntled reaction when I began introducing guys to the family. Of course, I didn't see that happening in the immediate future, but still. A girl could wish. I finally felt somewhat secure in my life since we had moved to South Carolina at the end of the summer. I had a bedroom that was completely unpacked, whereas in the past I'd always used moving boxes as my dresser. I would be graduating from Lincoln High in the spring instead of transferring to yet another high school. And best of all, I had friends who knew what my parents did for a living and still chose to be associated with me. Things were great, but there was still something missing from my life.

Or, more accurately, *someone* was missing.

I wanted to meet a guy, someone I could spend time with and share inside jokes with and curl up next to. Someone who would take me to the movies or out to eat and, most importantly, to the prom. More than anything, I wanted to go to prom, if only because it seemed like the most glamorously normal thing I could do.

"Girls?" Mom called from across the large room. Her voice echoed. "Any sign of him?"

Annalise stood up and looked out the window. "Not yet."

We were waiting for Leonard Zelden, a "renowned demonologist" and bestselling author who was already an hour late. My parents weren't happy about having to accommodate someone whose work conflicted with their own, but it was the only way they could get permission to film and research in the abandoned asylum. The owner of the building knew Zelden, and had promised us full access to the property on the condition that Zelden was present to document his own findings, which would undoubtedly find their way into yet another fat, glossy book.

My parents were known as debunkers; that is, they went into a "haunted" place and methodically uncovered evidence to prove that paranormal happenings were, in fact, just plain normal. They also worked under the theory that strange occurrences were often caused by harmless residual energy. Dad was a staunch believer in the effects of energy. Mom had been, too—until two months ago. Now she was beginning to research different theories about the paranormal, theories my

Dad absolutely rejected. It was causing some tension at home, and I hoped it wouldn't spill over into their documentaries. They had obviously decided to set aside their professional differences for the holiday, which I appreciated. It was weird enough to be checking the lights on a camera instead of on a Christmas tree, without the added stress of yet another parental disagreement to deal with.

Annalise sighed and wandered off to wallow in her longing for Mills while I tried to force my new phone to show signs of life. It was hopeless. Nothing could get through the thick concrete walls of Lake Sanitarium.

"Someone's here," Shane announced. We all stood at different windows and watched as a sleek white car slithered up the winding driveway and parked in front of the entrance. The graceful curves of Zelden's vehicle were a sharp contrast to our bulky van, which was painted black with the word *Doubt* stretched across it in tall silver letters. A young man got out of the driver's side and quickly opened the back door. An older man wearing a gray wool coat and hat emerged. He surveyed his surroundings and said something to the driver, who scurried to open the trunk.

"I already despise this guy," Dad muttered.

"He's not even helping with the camera," Shane pointed out. "What a tool."

"Be nice," Mom warned.

We heard footsteps thumping up the stairs and turned to greet our late guest. Zelden entered the room and immediately walked over to Mom, smiling wide and taking both her hands in his.

"Karen Silver! So lovely to finally meet you! I've heard marvelous things about you."

Mom was flustered. "Oh. Well, it's lovely to meet you, too."

Dad stepped forward. "Mr. Zelden, I'm Patrick Silver."

Zelden frowned. "It's *Doctor* Zelden, if you don't mind. I do hold a doctorate in theology, you know."

Dad gave him a stiff smile. "Of course."

Both my parents held doctorates in psychology, but they never referred to themselves as doctors. They said that title should be reserved for people who could actually save lives, not just write a thesis.

Zelden's assistant stumbled into the room, struggling under the weight of the video equipment. "Over there, Marcus," Zelden said in an unconcerned voice. He turned back to my mother. "Good assistants are *so* difficult to acquire," he said, winking. "Marcus has been with me for two years, and I'm still training him."

Mom nodded. "Dr. Zelden, I'd like to introduce you to our daughters." Annalise and I stepped forward, but Zelden was looking at Shane, who was positioning the tripod.

"Is that on?" he asked.

Shane grunted yes, and Zelden positioned himself directly in front of the camera. "As you can see, I travel without an entourage," he said, his voice louder. "I believe the pursuit of truth is a somewhat solitary calling, and, even though my devoted fans have often offered to help me with my research, I choose to focus purely on the work, with only minimal distractions." He glanced at me and Annalise.

"Our daughters are not a distraction," Dad said, clearly insulted. "They've been assisting us since they learned to walk."

Zelden smiled. "Of course. Now, where should we begin?"

While Marcus the Assistant made trips up and down the stairs to retrieve cameras, candles and coffee for his boss, Zelden and my parents went on a tour of the building to get a "feel for the energy." Shane followed with his video camera. Annalise and I stayed behind with Marcus.

"Merry Christmas," Annalise said to him as he hunched over a camera.

He looked up. "I'd forgotten that was today."

"How could you forget Christmas?" I asked.

Marcus shrugged. "Dr. Zelden doesn't celebrate the traditional holidays."

"No kidding." I was ticked that we were spending the day researching. It had been Zelden's decision to work on December twenty-fifth. While my parents usually scheduled something around the holiday, we rarely spent the actual day doing anything besides lounging around in a hotel watching classic movies and eating too much fudge. I studied Marcus as he pulled fat white candles from a cardboard box. He looked to be about college age, and was dressed like his boss: dark dress pants and a white-collared shirt with a tie. Again, it was a stark contrast to my family. We were wearing jeans and sweatshirts beneath our heavy coats.

I offered to help Marcus set up, but he firmly rebuffed me, saying that Dr. Zelden expected things to be done precisely.

"No offense," he said. "It's just that I can't allow any mistakes. It could interfere with his process."

I knelt down on the cold floor next to him. "What is his process?" I knew a little about Zelden's work, but it was mainly through what I'd heard my parents say, and none of it was flattering. They saw him as a complete fraud, although Zelden's book sales indicated that many people believed the opposite. He claimed to contact demons who resided in people's homes or businesses and "send them back to their place of origin." My parents scoffed at not only the concept of demons, but also the idea that one could summon and control something supposedly so powerful.

Marcus considered my question as he arranged the candles in a circle on the floor. "He's very guarded about the process. I don't completely understand it, and I've watched him work hundreds of times." He stood up and surveyed his work, then knelt down again to move a candle so it was perfectly aligned with the others. "The spirits speak through him," he continued. "His entire body changes. His voice becomes something otherworldly. It's fascinating."

"It sounds, uh, fascinating," I said.

Marcus smiled. "It's okay if you don't believe in it. You will, though. Before today is over, you'll get it."

I seriously doubted that Zelden's performance would convince me of anything other than his acting abilities, but I nodded. Marcus stood up.

"Is that them?" he asked, looking toward the doorway. "That was quick."

I followed his gaze but didn't see anything. "They're probably on another floor by now."

He frowned. "I heard voices."

"I don't hear anything."

Marcus returned to his work and I wandered over to Annalise, who was blowing into her hands to warm them up.

"What'd Marcus have to say?" she asked.

I shrugged. "Nothing much. He says we'll be amazed by Zelden's process."

"Unlikely." She looked around. "Where are they? I want to get this thing over with so we can go somewhere that actually has heat."

The group returned ten minutes later, Zelden leading the way. "Are we ready?" he asked Marcus.

"Yes, sir."

"Very well, then. May I have everyone gather around the candles?"

He wasn't really asking, I thought, as I lowered myself onto the ice-cold cement floor. Zelden was sitting on a pillow, of course. We formed a small circle with a stout white candle sitting directly in front of each one of us, but before we could begin, Zelden rearranged us so that Mom was on his left and Annalise was on his right. Dad looked less than pleased, but Mom shot him a glance before he could complain. We joined hands. Shane and Marcus stood behind us with their cameras.

"Close your eyes and breathe deeply," Zelden instructed in a melodic, soothing voice. "Allow yourself to feel the energy surrounding us, and know that the candle in front of you will keep you from harm."

I could almost feel Dad's disbelief as I held his hand. One small candle couldn't even keep us warm, much less safe, and the only thing I could feel was the cold seeping through my thick coat and Lincoln High sweatshirt.

Minutes passed. Zelden remained quiet, his eyes closed. The strange silence was beginning to become uncomfortable, and I was keenly aware of the wind howling outside and the hard iciness of the floor beneath me. It would have been polite, I thought, if Zelden had brought cushy pillows for all of us to sit on, but I knew his formal manners were just part of an act. My parents had taught me that true courtesy meant making sure the people around you were comfortable, a concept that was clearly beyond Zelden's comprehension.

I was squirming a little in a useless attempt to get more comfy when I heard the moaning. I stiffened, and Dad squeezed my hand more tightly. I opened my eyes. The low, steady sound was coming from Zelden. His head was tilted back, his mouth gaping. Everyone's eyes were open now. We watched as Zelden swayed his head from side to side as if fighting with something. His moaning became more guttural, almost like a growl, and his eyes rolled back in his head.

"Who dares disturb my sanctuary?" Zelden's voice was deep and menacing, and although I thought it was creepy, it was nowhere near "otherworldly," as Marcus had predicted.

"Who are you?" Mom asked.

"I am the Guardian of the Gate."

"The gate to where?"

Zelden groaned and writhed some more. Dad tensed his grip on my hand, and when I looked over at him, I saw that his lips were pursed in an attempt to keep from laughing. I had to look away quickly so I wouldn't catch a case of the giggles, as well.

"I guard the entrance to another realm, a place of pain, a continent of evil."

Dad coughed. I knew he was trying hard to keep from bursting with laughter. I also knew it wasn't really working. He was going to lose it and ruin our chances of filming some decent footage inside the asylum. I dug my nails into his palm, hoping that a pinch of pain would keep him from falling apart. Mom glanced at us and figured out pretty fast that she needed to move things along more quickly.

"Why are you here?" she asked.

"I am here to prevent souls from moving on."

"How many souls reside in this place?"

"Thousands."

"Why are you keeping them here?"

"I keep them here because I can."

"Are you a demon?"

"Yes."

Mom was asking her questions in machine-gun style, firing a new one before Zelden could elaborate on his answers. Dad coughed again, I squeezed his hand, and Zelden, who perhaps sensed that we weren't playing the game by his rules, began to writhe some more. He roared and rocked back and forth as if trying to rid himself of something. After a few more dramatic convulsions, he slumped forward, careful to make sure his head rested on his hands. He was silent and still. We sat there, waiting for him to do something else.

"Dr. Zelden?" Marcus was still filming, but he sounded genuinely concerned about his boss. "Dr. Zelden? Are you okay?"

Zelden abruptly sat up, gasping for breath. He looked around at us. "What happened?"

"You made contact, sir," Marcus said. His voice was tinged with admiration.

Dad stood up. He was coughing hard and trying to conceal his smile with his hand. "Just need some air," he sputtered as he practically ran to the door.

"Yeah, me, too." Shane carefully set down his camera. "That was, uh, intense."

We could hear their footsteps as Dad and Shane scurried down the stairs, the creak of the heavy front door and then the howl of their laughter as they stood outside. Mom cleared her throat and turned to Zelden.

"Do you remember anything?"

I knew she was just trying to be kind, but Zelden seemed to think that she believed his show. He sat up straighter, adjusted his collar and adopted his professional air.

"No, I'm afraid not. Once I give myself over to the other side, my mind goes blank."

"You said you were a demon," Annalise said. She was nearly shouting, trying to drown out the laughter still coming from outside.

Zelden nodded. "I suspected as much. Demons often claim places like this as their own. Here, they have access to many

trapped souls." He turned to Marcus. "We will need to per-
form a cleansing ceremony. Gather what we need from the
trunk."

Marcus flicked off his camera and left. I blew out the candles
while Mom and Annalise talked with Zelden. When Dad and
Shane returned from their laughing fit, Mom glared while
Zelden completely ignored them.

Dad clapped his hands together. "So. What's next?"

"We're going to participate in a cleansing ceremony," Mom
informed him.

"Sounds great. What can we do to help?"

"You can follow us," Zelden said stiffly. He turned to me.
"Wait here. Inform Marcus that we will be setting up in the
first-floor kitchen. I believe it may function as a portal to the
other realm."

"The demons crawl out of the oven," Annalise whispered
to me as she passed.

I looked at Mom. She nodded at me, so I stood where I was
while the others went downstairs. After they left I gathered
up the candles and placed them in the cardboard box I had
seen Marcus remove them from. I heard the front door open
and the echo of footsteps as Marcus hurried up the stairs.

"Where is everyone?" He sounded panicked.

"Kitchen. Don't worry, I'll help you with the rest of the
stuff and then we can join them."

Marcus frowned. "I'm not supposed to let anyone near Dr.
Zelden's equipment."

I hoisted the box of candles in my arms. "Trust me, I've
handled more sophisticated gear than this."

I began making my way to the door. I was walking past
Marcus when my shoulder accidentally brushed against his.
Before I could take another step I felt an intense pressure on
my arm.

"Ow!" I dropped the box, sending the candles flying across the floor. Marcus was gripping my arm. It felt like he was trying to push his fingers all the way through my flesh. I was simply startled at first, but that feeling almost immediately gave way to panic as the pain in my arm intensified.

"You have pushed back the curtain too far," Marcus said.

Only, it wasn't really Marcus. A voice was coming from his mouth, but it wasn't his voice. In fact, my first thought was that it wasn't even a *human* voice. It wasn't low and deep, like Zelden's idea of how a demon should sound. Instead, it was something between a hiss and a whisper, neither male nor female.

It was, quite simply, otherworldly.

And not a good world.

I tried to pull away. Marcus's gaze was fixed on me, but his eyes looked strange, like the blackness of his pupils had spread and swallowed the rest of his eyeballs. I tried to pull away, but his grip was cement. I knew if he squeezed any harder, my arm would break.

"Who are you?" I croaked. The pain was making me dizzy.

"I am the Watcher."

I knew I needed to scream. If I was loud enough, I was sure the sound would reach my parents in the kitchen. My legs gave out and I sank to the floor. Marcus was still clenching my arm, but now he was slowly twisting it as he dug his fingers into my flesh. I was fairly certain that the sensation was similar to getting shot in the arm. His fingers were five hot bullets.

"You have pushed back the curtain too far," Marcus repeated. "There is a price to be paid."

I tried screaming. I opened my mouth, but I was only able to gasp in pain. Black spots whirled in front of my eyes. With my free hand, I groped around the floor for something, anything. My hand closed around the fat base of one of the candles.

"Time is against you. You must pay," Marcus said. "You have pushed…"

I slammed the candle into his cheek. He flinched, and his grip on me loosened. The color immediately began to return to his eyes. I yanked my arm free and dragged myself out of his reach, cradling my throbbing arm in my lap.

"What happened?" he asked, looking dazed.

"Who are you?" I demanded as I tried to suck in oxygen.

Marcus looked around as if he had no idea where he was. "What's going on?"

I felt sick from the pain in my arm. "You might want to cover your ears."

"What? Why?"

"Nothing personal," I said, taking a deep breath. "But I'm going to start screaming now."

# two

I took my time walking down the hill to Avery's house. I was happy to be home after two weeks away, to return to the warm familiarity of our neighborhood. It was a young subdivision filled with nearly identical two-story houses colored in varying shades of beige siding. Every yard boasted exactly one tree, every driveway held two cars. I smiled as I approached Avery's house, with its narrow porch and tall topiaries.

She flung the door open before I could ring the doorbell. "You're back!" she squealed. Her wide smile quickly dissolved when she saw my arm. "What happened?"

I gave her a careful hug. "It's a long story. Let's go upstairs."

We went to her room, a calm oasis of perfectly matching furniture and pale pink walls. I sat down on her bed while she grabbed a floor pillow.

"Tell me everything," she said as she pulled her long blond hair back into a ponytail and sat cross-legged on the pink carpet.

I looked down at my arm, which was swaddled in a navy-blue sling. "Would you believe me if I told you that this is the result of a paranormal problem?"

"Yes." Avery was one of the few people in my life who knew nearly everything about my parents and the strange things that sometimes occurred as a result of their chosen profession. "Of course I believe you. Now, start from the beginning."

I began with Lake Sanitarium and Zelden's little perfor-mance. When I got to the attack, I had to pause. Describing the way Marcus had pulled and twisted my arm brought back a memory of pain so real I could almost feel it. Avery listened, her brow furrowed.

"What happened afterwards?" she asked.

"It was chaotic," I said, remembering how my mother had appeared in the doorway before I had finished screaming. She must have flown up the stairs. "I thought Dad and Shane were going to murder Marcus."

I explained that there's not much you can do after being involved in an otherworldly attack, particularly when your assailant has no recollection of the event. I had spent the rest of Christmas Day in the hospital having my arm x-rayed and enduring a hundred questions from concerned nurses who kept eyeing Dad as if he were the culprit. I'd probably think that, too, if I was an outsider looking in. Dad was a wreck. He was convinced that Marcus had assaulted me in some strange defense of his boss's honor.

"I knew Zelden had it out for me," Dad muttered as he paced the emergency room. "I just had no idea he would send his assistant after one of my daughters."

"It wasn't him," I protested. "It was something inside of him."

I could tell Mom and Annalise believed me. Every time I looked over at them from my hospital bed they were huddled in the corner, sharing their whispered thoughts. Of course, "a demon mauled me" wasn't the excuse we gave to the hospital staff. I invented a convoluted tale about how I was helping to load our van when I slipped on some ice, causing the heavy camera equipment to land directly on my arm, which had somehow twisted in the process. I thought it was very clever, but the doctor was obviously suspicious. He made me repeat my sad story a dozen times as he examined the X-rays and determined that I suffered from a torn ligament. "At least it's not a fracture," he said as he gingerly secured my bruised and swollen arm with the sling and prescribed painkillers.

"Get some rest," he advised. "And no heavy lifting for at least six weeks."

Zelden had wisely decided to avoid Dad, but he was skulking around the hospital trying to pry information from Annalise anytime she left my side to get ice. She told me that Zelden seemed more concerned about a potential lawsuit than my well-being.

"And Dad's angry enough that he would consider hauling him to court," Annalise confided. "He's been trying to get ahold of his lawyer, but since it's Christmas, he's not having any luck."

"Where's Marcus?" I asked.

"He's not here." Annalise patted my hand. "Zelden sent him back to the hotel."

I felt relieved. Even though I knew Marcus was not a maniac, I wanted distance from him.

Finally, I was released from the emergency room. It was past midnight, and Christmas was officially over. Annalise guided me into the van. "How are you feeling?" she asked as she carefully buckled the seat belt for me.

"I think the painkillers are kicking in," I mumbled. I was

exhausted, the combination of a long day and the medications finally taking effect.

I laid my head on Annalise's shoulder and let my eyes close. Trying to doze, I caught snippets of my parents' hushed conversation as Mom drove us back to the hotel.

"You cannot be so naïve, Karen," Dad said. "This was Zelden's revenge for years of our public criticism. He is trying to intimidate us. We should press charges."

"After we lied to the hospital? No. Besides, Charlotte was very clear. She doesn't believe Marcus knew what he was doing. Did you see him? The guy was absolutely traumatized."

Dad grunted. "And he should be. Are you really defending the man that sent your child to the hospital?"

Mom sighed. "I'm just saying that I trust Charlotte on this. And you should, too."

I stirred in my seat, desperately trying to find a position comfortable enough to sleep in. My parents stopped talking, and for the rest of the trip I drifted in and out of light consciousness. No matter what I did, though, I could not erase the image of Marcus's eyes as he gripped my arm. I knew it wasn't just a man that had grabbed me. It was something so much stronger. *The Watcher.* The Watcher of what? Of teenage girls forced to spend their holiday break filming cable TV specials? Or was the thing I had encountered some kind of energy confined to the asylum? I hoped so. I'd been followed home by spirits once in my life already, and once was more than enough.

*There is a price to be paid,* the voice had growled. I suspected that my injured arm was just the beginning of that price.

Avery sat back on her pillow. Her little dog, Dante, trotted over and curled up in her lap. "Okay. Here's what we'll do," she said, slipping into damage control mode. "We'll tell everyone it was a skiing accident. No one will think twice about it."

"Sounds good." I knew I could count on Avery to come up with a cover story. I did not want the details of my injury becoming public knowledge. Life as Charlotte Silver, daughter of moderately famous paranormal researchers Patrick and Karen Silver, could be difficult. It wasn't only that I'd grown up traveling constantly and had never really had a permanent place to call home. It was difficult because once people found out who I was and what my parents did for a living, they tended to see me differently. Worse, they treated me differently. But when we moved here for my senior year and I finally accepted that having a somewhat abnormal life wasn't all that bad, things seemed to improve. I had real friends and a stable routine and a room of my own.

Avery looked around the room and lowered her voice. "Any chance that whatever it was followed you here?"

I would have laughed if the same thought hadn't occurred to me. "No. And even if it did—" I leaned forward like I was about to reveal a secret "—whispering isn't going to prevent it from hearing you."

Avery rolled her eyes, but smiled. "I'm really glad you're back, Charlotte."

"Me, too. Now, what'd I miss?"

"Nothing nearly as exciting as what happened to you." She cringed. "I didn't mean it that way."

"Don't worry about it."

Avery leaped up, causing her dog to bark. "Sorry, Dante." She went over to her dresser, where she kept a dozen framed photographs, and plucked one from the middle. "I wanted to show you this." She handed me the silver frame. "It's from the Masquerade Ball."

I smiled at the picture in my hands. It was a group shot of

us, surrounded by our friends. We were laughing, our arms thrown around one another. I was looking right at the camera. Beside me, Avery beamed and Callie stuck out her tongue. Noah and some guys were behind us. Even Jared was in the picture, standing off to the side but revealing a rare smile.

"This is great. Have you seen Jared recently?"

"Just yesterday, actually." Avery sat down next to me. "He's doing really well. He's working on some project. He says it's related to Adam, but he won't tell me about it until it's finished," I handed the frame back to her and she ran her fingers over the glass. "The one-year anniversary of Adam's death is coming up," she said. "I think Jared's working on some kind of memorial."

Adam had been Avery's boyfriend and Jared's best friend until a car accident claimed his life. I knew that both were still dealing with Adam's loss, but they were moving forward.

"A memorial is a great idea," I said. "Let me know if I can help."

"When I figure out what Jared has planned, I'll let you know." She returned the picture to her dresser. "But right now we have other plans."

"Other plans?"

Avery turned and smiled. "There's a huge party tonight, and you're invited. We're celebrating New Year's in style."

I looked down at my sling. "I don't know. Navy-blue nylon isn't exactly a trend."

"I'll find you something to wear."

I trusted Avery's fashion sense, but I wasn't sure I was up to a crowded party, mainly because I'd never been to one. My parents' work meant that we had moved around a lot, usually before I could form solid friendships. This year had been different, though. Before I could tell her yes, Avery pulled an indigo blouse from her closet.

"This is perfect. The color will help your sling not stand out too much." She was still eyeing the blouse. "Noah will be there."

I looked up. "So?"

Avery shrugged. "So I just thought you might like to know, is all."

"We're friends, that's it. He made that pretty clear after the Masquerade Ball."

Too clear, in fact. We had shared a few slow dances, laughed over the watered-down fruit punch, and posed for pictures. But just when I thought things were going great, he pulled away—literally. We had been dancing, the white lights from the overhead disco ball swimming around us as we talked softly. But as soon as the song ended, he walked across the room to talk with some friends, and when the dance was over a few minutes later, he acted distant. After that, Noah continued to maintain a friendly but marked distance, making it clear that we were friends and absolutely, positively nothing else.

"Well, there will be other guys there," Avery said. "Callie thinks you and Harris Abbott would really hit it off. The party's at his house, so I'll make sure to introduce you."

I stood up. "I haven't even agreed to go and you're already setting me up with a football player?"

"I'm not setting you up," Avery said, rolling her eyes. "I'm simply introducing you to a nice guy. And you're going. What kind of friend would I be if I let you miss the biggest bash of our senior year?"

There was no winning this one and I knew it. "Fine. I'll go. But I don't want you forcing some guy to talk to me, okay?"

Avery squealed and ran over to give me a hug. "This is going to be great! You'll see, Charlotte. We're going to make this a year to remember. And it starts tonight."

With Avery's borrowed top in hand, I went home. I poked my head in Annalise's room, where an open suitcase sat on her bed. I could hear the shower running, so I went downstairs to find Shane. He was in the kitchen, whistling as he stood at the stove, making his famous omelets.

"Afternoon, kid," he sang out.

I poured myself some grapefruit juice and sat at the counter. "You're in a good mood today."

"Yes, I am. I'm back home, there's no snow—"

"I'll drink to that," I interrupted, raising my glass.

"And I have a date tonight."

"Ah, yes, the temptress Trisha."

Shane slid the omelet onto a plate and set it in front of me. "She is a temptress," he agreed. "But also a lady." He winked and sat down across from me. "So." He nodded toward my sling. "How you doing?"

"Good." Even though it was lunchtime, I happily devoured the eggs.

"Yeah? Because that's twice in two months now."

I knew what he was talking about. Before we had left for Charleston, I had been shoved—hard—by an unseen spirit wreaking havoc in our house. I had been hurt, but it wasn't nearly as serious as what had happened in Ohio.

I tried to smile. "I guess I'm just a paranormal punching-bag."

"I'm glad you can make jokes. Your parents are worried sick, though."

I looked toward the living room, where we kept all our video equipment and computers. "Are they home?"

"Nope. Your dad scheduled an early meeting with his lawyer. Your mom is out running errands."

I set down my fork. "His lawyer? Really? I told him it wasn't Marcus's fault, exactly." I honestly believed that Marcus had been just as shocked as I was after everything happened. He was sobbing in the corner when the ambulance arrived. I saw the pure confusion in his face, and the way he looked down at his hands as if they were not his own. No one was that good an actor. He had not been in control of what had happened. I knew it in my gut.

"It's not Marcus he's after," Shane informed me. "He blames Zelden. And he's worried that Zelden's going to try and profit off this."

I finished my omelet. "That wouldn't surprise me. I can totally see him using footage and staging some kind of reen-actment to support his demon theory."

After helping Shane tidy up the kitchen—a somewhat awk-ward and difficult task when you can use only one arm—I returned to my sister's room. Annalise was wearing her bath-robe, a towel piled on her head. Her back was to me as she folded clothes and neatly placed them in her open suitcase.

"Do you have to go back today?" I whined. Annalise went to college two hours south, in Charleston, and I knew classes didn't begin for another few days.

"Yes. I promised Mills I'd be back by dinnertime." She looked at my sling. "How's your arm?"

"Fine."

"Liar." She closed the suitcase and reached for another one. "Are Mom and Dad home?"

I plopped down in a chair and watched my sister pack. "Dad's meeting his lawyer and Mom is out running errands."

The corner of Annalise's mouth twitched when I mentioned Mom.

"What?" I demanded. "You know where she went, don't you? Tell me."

Annalise pushed a lock of wet hair out of her face. Even without makeup and with her long black hair hidden in a towel, my sister was still beautiful. "Mom went to see some friends," she said finally.

"What kind of friends?" I asked, even though I was pretty sure I knew the answer. Mom didn't maintain normal friendships. She never attended the potlucks or card games that other mothers participated in, and she claimed she didn't have time for the kind of female bonding that seemed to form over morning coffee and weekend shopping. If she had made a new group of friends, chances were they were the psychic variety Dad disapproved of.

"They're nice and normal, don't worry," Annalise said. "But they specialize in, you know, things."

"Right." I felt a little prick of jealousy that my sister had more knowledge about these people than I did. I knew that she'd recently gone with Mom on various "research trips," as she'd put it. I wanted to go, too, but Dad was completely against the idea. He knew Annalise was old enough to make her own decisions and he couldn't stop her, but he put his foot down when it came to me.

"She's too young and impressionable!" he yelled at Mom late one night. She had told me earlier in the day that we would be going on a research trip, but when Dad found out, he wasn't happy. I was supposed to be asleep, but they had been fighting in the kitchen for half an hour, their voices rising in small degrees with every sentence.

"She's almost eighteen! And since when have you considered either one of your daughters to be impressionable? They're more mature than some people twice their age!" I was pleased that Mom was sticking up for me, but I felt guilty about it, too. My parents wouldn't be fighting to begin with if it wasn't for me, which was a depressing thought.

In the end, when it became clear that neither one was going to budge, I solved the situation by declaring that I didn't really want to go. Dad smiled triumphantly and wrapped an arm around my shoulder while Mom simply pursed her lips together. Later, she came up to my room and sat on my bed.

"Thank you," she said.

I looked up from my French homework. "For what?"

"For understanding that your dad and I are going through a rough time right now." She smoothed out my wrinkled pillowcase. "I want you to know that it is not your job to be the peacemaker. Your dad and I need to work on some things, and we will. I don't want you to feel like you're caught in the middle." She smiled sadly. "Even so, I appreciate what you did." She walked over to where I was sitting at my desk and kissed my forehead. "We'll do better, I promise. No more yelling."

I almost broke down and sobbed in her arms. Since the incident in Charleston, things had felt so strained between my parents. They used a stiff courtesy with one another, like they were putting tremendous effort into getting along. Shane noticed it, too, but he said I had nothing to worry about.

"They've been married for over twenty years," he assured me. "And they've known each other even longer. Stuff like this happens in a marriage. It'll all blow over in a few weeks, you'll see."

But it didn't blow over. Something had changed between them, something that was at once so slight that most people wouldn't have noticed and yet so monumental that it was ripping them apart. And while the yelling did stop, I would often catch fragments of their fights as they whispered hoarsely at each other, as if they were arguing with the volume turned down.

Annalise pulled the towel off her head. Then she went over to her windows and opened the curtains. Something about that simple act made me nervous. It triggered the not-so-distant memory of the growling voice. *You have pushed back the curtain too far.* I shuddered a little. Part of me needed to understand what that unearthly statement meant, but a saner, more rational part of me didn't want to know. Whatever I'd encountered at the asylum seemed to have stayed in Ohio. I'd had no inkling of anything remotely paranormal since we'd left the building, and that had been five days ago. Maybe the Watcher was a powerless blob of extra-scary residual energy. Then again, residual energy didn't jump inside a living guy and make him attack an innocent girl, right?

*Unless I'm not so innocent.* My previous ghostly encounter in Charleston had left me with the nagging sense that I'd stepped across some invisible line. I'd set foot into another realm and shared a casual conversation with a girl who had died a hundred years earlier. It was the strangest, most intense experience I'd ever had—and one I hadn't told anyone about.

There was no way to explain it, really. Even if Mom and Annalise believed me, they would always wonder if I wasn't just a teeny bit mental. After all, I'd never shown any kind of psychic sensitivity in my entire life. And Dad would have flipped out.

No, I decided, it was best to keep it to myself, to dissect the incident on my own terms, in my own time. This meant that I thought about it constantly every night as I tried to fall asleep, turning my memories over and over like a stone in my head. At first, everything seemed so vivid, so real. I *knew* it had happened. But as the weeks passed and the feelings faded, I wondered: had it happened exactly as I remembered? Or had I mixed up reality with my dreams?

If I really had crossed an unseen threshold into the supernatural, shouldn't something about me be different? I waited to see if my venture to the other side would trigger a new, profound awareness. Would I be able to communicate with spirits?

Would I be accosted by creepy corpses? But two months had passed and nothing at all had seemed different about my life until the encounter with Marcus in Ohio.

"I don't think Dad knows," Annalise said as she rubbed at her damp hair. "About Mom's new friends, I mean. I heard her tell him last night that she was going to do some research today."

"So she's lying to him?" I began chewing at a fingernail.

"She's not *technically* lying. It's just that her research involves talking to psychics."

"Well, if Dad finds out, he'll *technically* go ballistic."

Annalise gave me a sympathetic look. "I know they've been fighting lately. I know it's hard for you because you're here and I'm at school. But it's Mom and Dad. They'll work it out, okay? I know they will."

She walked down the hall to the bathroom while I stayed in her room. Everyone was telling me that things would be fine. I seemed to be the only person who didn't feel the same way. And my sister had just clarified the reason why: I was home. Annalise was away at school and Shane always returned to his apartment, but I shared a house with my parents and was with them more than anyone else. I saw the way they were avoiding one another. I heard their tense voices. And I suspected that Dad was sleeping on the sofa downstairs, but he was always up so early that I wasn't completely sure.

As I pushed myself out of the chair, I accidentally put too much pressure on my arm. I gasped at a sudden surge of pain and sat back down. The doctor had diagnosed me with a severe sprain and a torn ligament. I would have to wear the sling until February. At first, the sling hadn't bothered me. In fact, I'd thought a little compassionate attention from people might be a good thing. Maybe someone would help carry my books to class, bring me my lunch and that kind of thing.

But then I'd caught my parents sneaking glances at me and I'd understood that each of them believed something totally different had caused my injury. The sling provided a constant reminder that they no longer saw eye-to-eye.

I'd thought I was lucky that my arm hadn't been broken in the attack.

Now I worried that the attack was breaking my family.

# three

I wondered how long we had until the police arrived. Avery, Noah and I had been at the New Year's Eve party for less than fifteen minutes, and I was fairly certain that we had only fifteen more before the cops arrived with their sirens blaring. The music was so loud we heard it when we parked Avery's car at the end of the cul-de-sac, the thumping bass mixed with the squeals of excited girls and hollers of drunk, stumbling guys.

"Relax," Avery yelled over her shoulder as she maneuvered through the crowded living room. I held on to the back of her shirt, afraid I would lose her in the crushing mass of people and hoping no one accidentally slammed into my injured arm. Behind me, Noah had one hand placed firmly on the small of my back. I was acutely aware of the warmth of his palm pressed into me. I liked it, but I knew he was only doing it so he wouldn't lose me in the crowd.

Noah had arrived at my house earlier in the evening with his mom in tow. Trisha was there to see Shane, of course, and Noah was meeting me and Avery so we could drive to the party together. I wanted to run over and give Noah a hug, but held back. I wasn't sure if we were the kind of friends who did that, and I didn't want to create any awkwardness between us.

When Noah saw my arm in a sling, he smiled. "Rough Christmas?"

Dad used the opportunity to tell his side of the story once again, emphasizing Zelden's rudeness and describing Marcus as a thug. His version was much more intense than my recollection, but Trisha and Noah presented an interested audience. When Dad got to the part where Marcus attacked me, I quietly left the room to apply my lipstick. When I returned, Dad was recounting our trip to the emergency room.

"And now Charlotte has to suffer for five more weeks until her arm heals," he was saying.

I didn't consider myself to be suffering too terribly, although getting dressed took longer and required cautious attention. I didn't contradict Dad, though. He was on a roll. While he droned on about meeting with his lawyer, I went over to Noah.

"Ready for tonight?" I asked. "Avery says it's going to be huge."

Noah just pursed his lips and nodded in response. I guessed he was as tired of Dad's lengthy story as I was.

"There should be consequences when a child is assaulted," Dad proclaimed.

I winced at his referral to me as a child. "Okay, Dad. Can we drop it, please?"

All I wanted was to go to a party with my friends, not relive the attack. And Dad's attitude that he was somehow embarking on a crusade for justice was getting to me.

"Charlotte." Dad walked over to me and kissed the top of my head. "I understand that you're scared, and that's okay. Let me do the worrying for you. I know how Zelden operates."

"I told you, it wasn't Zelden! It wasn't even Marcus."

Dad shook his head. "You don't get it, and that's fine." He offered a rueful smile to Shane and Trisha. "Ignorance is bliss, I suppose."

"You're saying that I'm ignorant?" My voice rose an octave.

Mom hurried over. "That's not what your father is saying." She gave Dad a disapproving glare. He shrugged and went to the kitchen. As far as he was concerned, the conversation was over, but my anger at being treated like a child was only beginning to boil.

"You okay?" Noah stood in front of me with his hands shoved into his pockets. I took a deep breath and tried to calm myself.

"My dad acts like he was the one who was hurt. He didn't see it happen. He doesn't know." A car honked in the driveway. "Avery's here," I said, walking to the front door. "I need to get out of this house."

Noah said good-bye to his mom while I bounded down the front steps and flung open the passenger door.

"Ready to welcome the new year?" Avery asked.

"More like ready to say good-bye to the old one."

More than half the school appeared to have shown up for the party, which was being held at Harris Abbott's massive, Tudor-style house that overlooked the ninth hole of a golf course. His parents were away, Avery explained, and as long as we volunteered to help clean up the following afternoon, it was ours.

Avery made her way to the kitchen, where a group of guys wearing blue football sweatshirts circled a shiny keg. She greeted each one of them by name, then stepped slightly to the side. "This is Noah, and you guys know Charlotte, of course."

Thanks to my parents' documentaries airing throughout the month of October, everyone in town knew who I was. Meanwhile, I was still struggling to remember the first names of all the people who sat at my lunch table.

The football players handed us oversized plastic cups filled with warm, foamy beer. Avery started talking to a few of the guys while I tried to have a conversation with Noah, but I had to practically scream in his ear and then I couldn't make out his response. I spotted Callie across the room and waved, but she didn't see me. I also caught a glimpse of Jared, who was looking in our direction. He nodded at me before disappearing in the crowd.

I tried to capture Avery's attention. I thought maybe we could find another place to go, a room that wasn't quite so tightly packed with people, but she had moved a little farther away. When I turned back around, Noah was gone, too, squeezed out by the crowd trying to maneuver closer to the keg.

The music grew louder. I tried to inch my way out of the kitchen, which felt too stuffy and reeked of sweat and beer. My shoes kept sticking to something on the floor, and I desperately wanted to escape into the cold night air, but I was wedged in between one of the football players and the oven.

"You want to get out of here?" I could barely turn my head to see the guy who was talking in my ear, but I nodded, and a second later was being nudged out of the kitchen and through a set of French doors that opened onto a wide deck. Once outside, I took a deep breath.

"You looked like you needed a little fresh air. You okay?"

"I'm good." I finally got a chance to look at my rescuer. "Thanks for getting me out of there. I'm not a big fan of crowds."

The guy standing across from me was wearing a blue football sweatshirt, just like the others standing around the keg. He wore his brown hair buzzed close to his scalp, giving him an almost military look, but his wry smile made him seem much more approachable.

"I know what you mean. I'm okay with lots of people as long as they're sitting in the bleachers. I don't know why I let the guys talk me into hosting this thing."

"Maybe because this is the only house big enough to hold the entire school?"

He chuckled. "Maybe. By the way, I'm Harris." He motioned toward my sling. "I'd try to shake your hand, but it looks like that might be a bad idea."

I laughed. "It might be."

"What happened?"

I panicked for half a second before I remembered the story Avery and I had come up with. "Skiing accident."

Harris whistled. "That's rough."

I could tell that he wanted to ask me more about it, so I tried to steer him off course. "So this is your house?"

"Yeah." He glanced behind him, where someone was flicking the lights on and off. The windows hummed along with the bass of the stereo inside. "My folks are in Atlanta for two more days, though, so I'm not worried."

"What about your neighbors? Aren't you afraid they might call the cops?" I hoped I didn't sound too paranoid, but I'd never been to a party this huge, and the stereo had now reached deafening levels.

Harris waved his hand. "There's not that many houses on this street, really," he said. "And most everyone is away for New Year's. That's why I'm at home, actually. I've been dog-sitting for half my neighbors all week."

He led me to a built-in bench nestled into one corner of

the cedar deck and I sat down, grateful to relax. A few people were standing outside, mainly couples absorbed in conversation. Bright light poured from the French doors and I looked over, hoping to catch a glimpse of Avery or Noah.

"You're good friends with Avery, aren't you?" Harris asked.

"I am, yeah." When I'd moved to town in August, Avery and I had immediately become friends.

"She seems to be doing really well lately." Harris ran a finger around the rim of his plastic cup. "Better than she was last year, I mean."

I knew he was referring to Adam's death. "You played on the team with Adam, right?"

Harris nodded. "He was a great guy."

I wasn't sure what to say. We were quiet, which was a little awkward, but not too much. It was cold, so I squeezed my good arm against me. Harris noticed.

"Do you want my sweatshirt?" Before I could protest, he was peeling it off and wrapping it around my shoulders. It was soft and smelled faintly woodsy. His cologne, I thought. Or maybe an aftershave.

"Thanks," I murmured. It was the first time a guy had ever done something for me that was so...chivalrous. I couldn't help but smile.

"Ready to go back in?" He was dressed only in a thin white T-shirt, which allowed me a good look at his sculpted arms and broad chest. Obviously, all those football practices had paid off.

"Do we have to?" I wanted a few more moments of sitting outside, next to Harris, without having to scream in order to be heard.

He leaned back and stretched his legs out. "Nah. We can

stay out here for a while." He looked up at the black sky. "On one condition, though."

"What's that?"

"You have to stare at the stars with me."

I smiled. "I think I can do that."

We spent the next half hour gazing upward. Harris pointed out different constellations to me. I only knew the Big Dipper, but he knew many more.

"How do I know you're telling me the truth?" I asked at one point. "I mean, you could be making these up."

"I could." He looked at me. "Guess you'll just have to trust me."

I tried to wrap his sweatshirt around me more tightly, but it was difficult to do with only one usable hand. "Here," Harris said. "Let me help you." He moved forward, putting his arm around me, and began to pull me toward him. As he wrapped the shirt around my shoulders, I breathed in the scent of his neck. He definitely wore cologne, but it was light. I immediately loved it. Harris didn't sit back after he had secured his shirt around me. Instead, he moved a little closer. Now I didn't need the sweatshirt—I was growing warmer by the second just sitting with him, wondering if he would try to kiss me. When I looked at him, our faces were almost touching.

"Harris!" The French doors swung open and one of the football players stepped onto the deck. "We're out of ice!" he hollered.

Harris sighed. "I guess hosting-duty calls." He stood up. "There's more in the basement freezer," he told the guy. "I'll be there in a minute."

He turned back to me. "Sorry about that. You ready to go inside?"

"I guess." I wasn't really ready to endure the onslaught of people and noise. I just wasn't used to it. My life had consisted mainly of traveling with my family and Shane and exploring empty buildings at night. Silence was a familiar friend.

"You know, there's another party across the street," Harris said as we walked across the deck. "It's not nearly as crowded."

I was surprised. "Really?"

"Yeah. Well, the thing is, it's kind of, um…weird?"

I paused. "What kind of weird?"

Harris opened the French doors and I was hit by a blast of warm air, intense lights and raucous music. "Actually, I think you might like it."

While Harris searched for ice I caught up with Noah and Avery, who were back in the kitchen. The stereo was not quite as loud as it had been earlier, and the crowd was not so densely packed.

"Nice shirt," Noah muttered when he saw me.

Avery grinned. "I saw you go outside with Harris. You've been gone awhile."

I knew I was blushing. "We weren't gone that long. He was just being nice."

"Right," Avery teased. "Nice."

It felt strange to talk about it with Noah standing right there, but I wasn't sure why. I definitely wanted to tell Avery everything, but later, when we were alone. I told her and Noah about the party across the street. "What do you think? You want to check it out?"

Avery shrugged. "I guess. But I thought everyone from school was here. I haven't heard anyone mention another party."

"I'm in," Noah said, but he didn't sound enthusiastic about it.

After Harris returned, Avery, Noah and I followed him through the living room and out the front door. As we crossed the street, which was still packed with cars, Harris gave us only a few details. "It's Gwyn's house," he explained. "Her family is away, too."

I knew the name—Gwyn was also a senior—but couldn't quite picture her face. I wasn't sure how I felt about entering someone's house when they weren't there, but Avery didn't say anything, so neither did I. Still, I felt edgy. I had no idea what we were walking into.

From the outside, the brick colonial house was completely dark. Not even the porch light glowed. Harris knocked on the front door twice before slowly turning the handle.

"Follow me," he whispered.

It was difficult to see inside the pitch-black entryway, but my eyes quickly adjusted and I could make out a fuzzy, flickering light at the end of the hallway. Harris walked confidently toward the light while the rest of us followed more slowly. The light became brighter and I could hear a girl's voice. It was low and steady, like she was telling a story. Finally, Harris stepped through a rounded archway into a den.

"I thought you might need some more," he said to the group of people sitting on the floor. I realized that the light was coming from dozens of white votive candles arranged in a circle.

A girl I knew vaguely from my history class smiled. "Thank you, Harris." She looked at Avery, Noah and myself. "You're right. We could use some fresh victims."

# four

Everyone knows a ghost story. Everyone knows someone who knows someone who has seen or heard or felt something that just didn't make sense, something unexplainable. For some reason, these stories tend to take place at night, in dark and isolated spots. Those stories never scared me. I understood that nine times out of ten there was a rational explanation behind the occurrences that tended to freak other people out. I knew that you could walk away, and leave the supernatural behind you.

For the most part.

But the things that could follow you home, the things that weren't looking for a home but rather a living person to reside with—well, those stories were creepier. Thankfully, most of the tales being told around the flickering candles were garden variety ghost stories: something white and hazy descending a staircase at midnight, the outline of an old woman gliding through a wall and more than a few about footsteps heard pacing around empty attics.

Everyone knew a ghost story. And, according to the rules of the game, everyone had to share their most terrifying tale.

Or else.

After the initial uneasy feeling of coming across a group of our classmates sitting in a candlelit circle had worn off, I was able to focus on Gwyn, the girl from my history class. She was long and lean and wore her dark brown hair cut in a sharp bob that framed her face. I don't think we'd ever spoken to one another. She played on the girls' basketball team and had always seemed kind of serious in class, but that was all I knew about her. Harris had said her family was away. I wondered why she had chosen to stay behind in the huge house.

"The rules are simple," Gwyn told us. The group of about a dozen people made room for us, and I sat in between Harris and Avery, with Noah sitting on the other side of Avery. "You have to describe, in as much detail as possible, an unexplained or paranormal experience that you or someone very close to you has experienced. After you finish your story, light a candle in front of you." Gwyn waved a hand over the twenty or so candles still unlit. "Our goal is to tell a hundred stories and light a hundred candles. After all the candles have been lit, we will have a hundred spirits in the room with us."

"And then what?" Noah asked. I detected a note of skepticism in his voice.

Gwyn sat in a lotus position and folded her hands. "And then we watch what happens."

*We'll be watching for a long time,* I thought. *Nothing is going to happen.* I wished Harris hadn't brought me here. Not only was it a waste of time, but it was exactly the kind of thing my parents frowned upon. More than frowned, actually. They basically forbid Annalise and I to ever participate in games like this, if you could call them games. Dad thought participation in any kind of weird ritual had the potential to hurt our family's reputation as scientific debunkers. Mom would be angry, too, but for different reasons. She believed that while games like Ouija boards weren't "real," they could stir up dormant energy. Basically, she felt you could open yourself up to negative energy, inviting it into your life. Dad agreed with this, but didn't believe it as wholeheartedly as Mom. Either way, they would be more than a little disappointed if they knew I was here.

I thought about Dad calling me a kid, and the way he had droned on and on about Ohio. I felt strangely pleased with myself for participating in something that he would be furious about if he knew. *Ignorance is bliss,* he'd said. Fine. I would apply his logic: if he didn't know I was delving into stupid games, then he wouldn't be hurt. Not that I cared if he was.

"It's good that you guys are here," someone said. I looked over and saw Callie, a friend of Avery's and mine. "We were running out of stories," she explained.

Harris reached toward an unlit candle. "I'll go first."

"Remember," Gwyn said. "It has to be a true story, something that actually happened to you or someone you know. And it's better if it actually happened to you. One fake story can mess up the whole thing." She looked directly at me. "And we're not here to judge. We simply listen. No questions. Understood?"

Gwyn stared at me. I stared back until I couldn't take it any longer and looked down. It felt like she was accusing me of something.

"We get it." Harris furrowed his brow. "This happened when I was little," he said. "My grandma had this dog. It was a white poodle and she loved it, treated it like her own kid. It would always claw at my legs under the dining room table when we ate dinner at her house, trying to get me to feed it scraps. I hated that because then my leg would be all scratched up afterwards." He paused. "Well, the dog got really old and died. A few months later, we were having dinner with my grandma and I felt this tugging at my pants. I looked down and there was nothing there. But it felt like the dog, like it was begging for food. That night, I was getting ready for bed and I saw it."

"The dog?" someone asked.

Gwyn immediately shushed them. "No questions allowed," she hissed.

Harris shook his head. "Not the dog. My leg." He looked up. "My leg was covered with long red scratches." After a moment, he leaned forward and lit his candle, then pushed the votive toward the center of the circle and handed me the lighter.

I picked up a candle. "This is gonna be good," someone whispered. Suddenly, I wanted to leave. I could almost feel the expectations people had built for me and knew how they were waiting for me to come through, to tell them some ridiculously scary tale. Most of my stories weren't that scary, though. Not to me, at least. Most of the things I had witnessed could be explained.

"I'll tell one from when I was little, too," I began. I had to think another minute, which I guessed people interpreted as dramatic suspense, but really, I just needed to come up with something that truly was unexplained. Something distant, I thought. I did not want to bring up Charleston, and I was hoping that Avery and Noah wouldn't, either.

I cleared my throat. "Once, my sister and I were with our parents while they were investigating an old prison. It was daytime, and Annalise and I were walking down a hallway, just talking, when she stopped and touched the back of her hair. I was about to ask her what was wrong when I felt it, too." I looked around the circle of my classmates. They were all watching me. "I felt a hand tug my ponytail. Hard, like someone wanted my attention badly. My sister and I ran as fast we could to get out of there.

"The thing is, when I asked my sister what she had felt, she had a different story. Her hair wasn't pulled. Instead, she said it felt like someone's cold fingers lightly grazing the back of her neck."

Afterward, Annalise had demonstrated what the touch had felt like, and it still sent shivers down my spine. The sensation made me think of a tarantula climbing down my back. I lit my candle and added it to the circle. Then I passed the lighter to Avery, who started telling her story without hesitation.

"My mom and I were on vacation a few years ago. We used to always rent a bungalow near Myrtle Beach. One year, the house we were staying in felt weird. There was something not quite right, you know?" She tucked a lock of hair behind her ear. "The sink would turn on by itself, usually late at night, but sometimes in the daytime, too. We had a plumber come out and everything, but he couldn't find a problem. The faucet would start running, and it wouldn't stop until one of us got up and turned it off. We didn't go back to that house."

I tried to look around the room without moving my head much. About half the faces were familiar to me, mainly seniors I had classes with. I was surprised to see Bliss Reynolds sitting in the circle. Bliss and I had AV class together, and we weren't exactly friends. I was under the impression that she was not a believer in anything even remotely paranormal, but she was sitting there with three lit candles placed directly in front of her.

Noah was next. I cringed, wondering if the events of Charleston were about to be revealed to our classmates. If people heard about the Circle of Seven and the ethereal lights we had witnessed, I would be inundated with questions and the kind of odd and unwelcome attention I thought had been put to rest for a while.

"We've lived in the same house since I was a baby," Noah began. "And while I was growing up, we had the same neighbor. Her name was Agnes, and she used to babysit me while my mom was at work."

I felt relief as I listened to Noah. I was also curious. We'd had several discussions about the paranormal, but he'd never mentioned anything about his neighbor.

"Agnes was old, and we always made sure she was okay. My brothers would run errands for her and change light bulbs, stuff like that. In return, she was always giving us peaches." He smiled. "She grew peach trees in her backyard, and she'd can the fruit and make jam and preserves and pies. Her house always smelled like peaches.

"She got cancer and died five years ago. We all took it hard, my mom especially. About a month later, we were talking about her, and after a few minutes, we could smell peaches. It was the strangest thing because it was winter and we were inside and there was just no way, you know? It was like someone had sprayed peach air freshener in the room, it was so strong."

Noah reached for his candle. Before he lit it, he stopped. "It happened a few more times after that. We would be talking about her, and the room would smell like peaches. And once, when I was just *thinking* about her, it happened." He lit the candle. "But it hasn't happened in years. I think she went away."

Bliss reached across the circle, and Noah gave her the lighter. "Last year, I went with the girls' basketball team to a school about thirty miles from here for a game. I was covering the game for the school paper. It was raining really hard, and when we got to the school, the roof over the gym was leaking, and they were going to have to forfeit.

"We had to wait in the school library to see if we were going to play or not. Everyone was kind of grumpy. We were sitting there when we heard a thump. It sounded like something fell and hit the carpet, but we didn't see anything. Every few minutes, though, we'd hear another thump."

Everyone watched Bliss with the same solemn expression. I wondered how long they had been assembled here, telling their stories. It had to take hours to get through a hundred of them.

"One of the coaches came by to tell us the game was cancelled," Bliss continued. "He came in a different door than we had, so he passed by the bookshelves where we had heard the noises. He got upset. He started yelling at us about how we should respect school property. We had no idea what he was talking about, of course."

Bliss looked around the circle. "As we were leaving, we saw what he meant. There were books lying all over the floor between the stacks. Books that had come from some of the top shelves. And none of us had been anywhere near those shelves."

I thought Bliss was trying too hard to make her voice sound dramatic, but other people nodded and seemed impressed.

"But the really weird thing was that all of the books were open and turned to page fifty-five."

She lit her candle. I counted the remaining votives. There were eleven left, and I was glad we had arrived so late in the game. Sitting around coming up with stories was tough, but listening to a hundred? No, thanks.

The next few anecdotes involved incidents I'd heard about a thousand times. A boy claimed that he could hear a baby crying in the basement of his uncle's house. A girl felt like someone was following her up a staircase where she worked. Others knew people who had witnessed wispy white ghosts or felt cold spots in otherwise warm rooms.

As I listened, I automatically debunked these stories in my head. Most of them were caused by the environment where they took place. Old paint and different kinds of mold could trigger intense hallucinations or strong feelings in otherwise normal, healthy people. Bad wiring and electrical problems also contributed to unexplained anxiety or even the sensation that someone was standing close by. And nine times out of ten, cold spots were simply drafts that no one had detected before. I had helped my parents with literally thousands of investigations, and over ninety percent of the time, there was nothing truly paranormal about what was happening, even if it seemed really spooky. Of course, it only took one seriously supernatural incident to shake you to the bones.

Soon, only two candles remained. No one was volunteering, and I guessed it was because they'd already exhausted every story they knew. Gwyn had jokingly called us "fresh victims," but, as the silence stretched, I knew that everyone was counting on us to come up with the final two tales.

I pulled a candle toward me and described a memory from when I was younger and we lived in an old Victorian-era house. "The rocking chair would move by itself, like someone was sitting there," I explained. "It happened all the time, usually right after dinner."

As I lit my candle, I wondered if I had broken the rules of the game. I had told the truth, but Gwyn had asked for stories of the unexplained, and honestly, the rocking chair wasn't totally paranormal. According to my parents, it moved because of residual energy. People who had lived in the house long before us had probably owned a rocking chair. Someone had likely sat in that chair every day after dinner for years, until the basic, repetitive act of rocking became its own kind of energy, and that energy imprinted itself upon the house. There was no human spirit residing in our living room, merely a thread of the past replaying itself over and over.

One candle remained. I was ready for the game to be over so we could turn on all the lights and go back across the street to celebrate the New Year. We'd been sitting in the circle for about an hour, and I was more than ready to get up, stretch my legs and even return to the noise and chaos of Harris's house. It would feel normal, at least, to cram myself into a packed living room instead of listening to the quiet fears of others.

I was about to get it over with and take the last votive when someone else reached for it. I sat back and watched as Gwyn claimed the final candle.

"I've been saving this one for last," she said. I sat back on my hands, happy that I wouldn't have to tell another story and even happier that the game was nearly over. Next to me, Harris also sat back, his hand lightly brushing my own. I wondered if he'd touched me on purpose.

"My parents are renovating this house," Gwyn started. "It's over a hundred years old, so they're gutting the kitchen, replacing the roof, that kind of thing. It's taking forever."

It was a familiar beginning to me. Home renovations often triggered dormant energy, a phenomenon my parents investigated more than any other. Their inquiries usually concluded that whatever the homeowner was experiencing amounted to little more than residual energy being stirred up, almost like someone shaking a bottle of juice. In fact, my parents received so many calls about strange things happening during a remodeling project that they rarely examined them anymore unless something truly unique stood out. I wondered if Gwyn's parents had called mine.

"About a week after they started working on the house,

strange things began to happen," Gwyn continued. "Little things, at first, like furniture or papers being moved at night, so that when we woke up the next day they were in the wrong place. Sometimes we heard footsteps in the hallway, and once my dad heard muffled voices coming from the kitchen. The more work we did on the house, the more things happened."

I hoped Gwyn would hurry up. Nothing about her tale was all that unusual. I had to stifle a yawn as she went on to describe how her family took pictures that revealed orbs in the corner of the kitchen. Why people got worked up about small white balls of light in a photograph was beyond me. It was usually dust or bugs.

"Last month it got really bad," Gwyn said, her voice softer. "So bad, in fact, that my mom moved out." I sat up straighter, ready to hear about something other than random noise and minor movement.

"It was late at night, and we all heard sounds coming from downstairs, like furniture was being moved. My whole family went together—my parents and my brother and me—and sure enough, the dining room table had been pushed against a door." She paused. "That's when we saw the light. It was like someone was walking across the room holding a flashlight, but there was no one there, just the light. It glided right past us, and I felt a cold breeze when it did. Then I heard a voice. It was so clear and so close that for a second I thought my brother had said something, but it wasn't my brother's voice."

People were leaning forward, eager to hear the rest of the story. When Gwyn was silent for a second too long, a boy near her asked, "What did the voice say?"

Gwyn flicked on the lighter and held up the final candle. "It said, 'Thank you for pushing back the curtain.'"

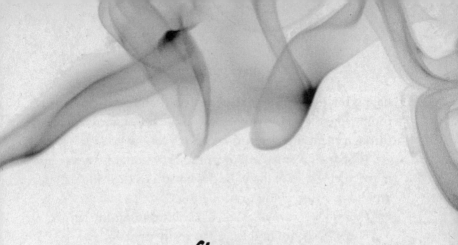

# five

"Are you sure he's not a serial killer?"

"Hello, Noah. Happy New Year to you, too." I leaned into the bathroom mirror to apply lip gloss while trying to balance the phone on my shoulder. The strange angle was aggravating my arm, though.

"Sorry. Hi, Charlotte. Happy New Year. Now, are you absolutely sure Shane isn't a serial killer?"

I used my pinkie finger to wipe a little excess gloss from my top lip. "Pretty sure."

Noah was constantly asking me about Shane, who was like an uncle to me. While I was happy that Shane was dating Trisha, Noah was miserable that his mom was now going out all the time.

"Because he fits the profile, you know. And he travels a lot, so he could have left behind dozens of corpses all over the country."

"Hmm. Well, that would explain the smell coming from his van."

Noah sucked in his breath and I laughed. "Kidding! Look, he's a nice, normal guy who's crazy about your mom. Be happy for them." I left the bathroom and returned to my room, where a pile of clothes lay on the bed. I started picking through them in a determined search for my good jeans.

"If Shane's so nice and normal, how come he never got married? He's, like, forty. And who spends their life driving around in a van trying to film ghosts?"

"Careful," I warned. "You're about to insult my family."

"Sorry," Noah mumbled. "I'm really tired."

I located the jeans and inspected them for obvious stains. "It's okay. I know how you feel."

It *had* been a late night. After all one hundred candles had been lit, we waited without speaking. Then Gwyn led us into her kitchen, which was still unfinished. While everyone else quietly inspected the cupboards and corners, I kept turning over Gwyn's story in my head. *Thank you for pushing back the curtain.* It gave me chills. What did it mean, exactly? Was it simply an eerie coincidence or was my experience in Ohio connected with Gwyn's experience at home? She had said it happened a month earlier, so whatever I encountered in Ohio could not have possibly followed me back to South Carolina.

I hoped.

"So, what did you think about that whole thing last night?" I asked.

Noah sighed. "I don't know. After what happened in Charleston, I'm kind of open to anything, but it seemed hokey. I didn't feel anything afterwards, did you?"

"I definitely didn't feel a hundred spirits in the room with us, if that's what you mean."

Still, I thought I had detected something. Despite my two recent supernatural experiences, I wasn't sensitive like some people. I never relied on my feelings alone, but I knew what to be aware of, and as the group of us stood in the kitchen, waiting, I tried to tune in and pay attention. Seconds after Gwyn finished telling her story, the candles all flickered in the same direction, as if responding to a slight breeze. The debunker in me immediately looked around to pinpoint the source, but I couldn't figure it out. The room was warm and stuffy and still. No one had moved, and even if someone had exhaled deeply, the candles were scattered in such a way that not all of them would have been affected. In fact, Noah coughed a moment later, and only a couple votives flickered at all.

There was something not quite right, something I couldn't define, and it was more than just a feeling. It was like my brain was trying to alert me to something out of place. I continued to scan the room, hoping to identify what was wrong. Most of my classmates were focusing on the corner where Gwyn had said the cold light had passed. A few had closed their eyes. Bliss was also looking around, and for a split second, our eyes met. She frowned and turned away.

I tried to move closer to Gwyn. I needed to talk to her about the voice she had heard. But every time I came within a few steps of her, she moved away, almost as if she was trying to avoid me.

When the hallway clock chimed eleven, the spell seemed to break and people began to move toward the front door.

"It may take a while," Gwyn said. "But something *will* happen. You'll see."

There was a general disappointed grumbling in response. After all, most of the group had sat around for hours hoping to witness something unusual, something caused by the hundred spirits brought forth by their hundred stories. I was just happy to escape the house and return to the party across the street. It was still loud and crowded, but at least it felt normal. Harris stayed at my side for the rest of the night, and we counted down the waning seconds of the year with the rest of the packed room. As the fireworks in Times Square erupted on the TV screen, Harris wrapped both arms around my waist and pulled me close.

"Happy New Year," he whispered. Before I could respond, his lips were pressed against mine. I don't know why I was surprised—we were surrounded by couples ringing in the new year with a celebratory embrace—but I was. The kiss seemed to end before I fully registered what was happening, but Harris kept his arms around me in a way that announced to the rest of our classmates that we were together. The fireworks exploding on TV were nothing compared to what was igniting inside of me.

I checked the clock on my nightstand. It was just after noon. "Avery's going to be here soon," I informed Noah.

"Mom's still sleeping in. Shane didn't bring her home until almost three this morning. I was about to call the cops. And she didn't even tell me where they were all night, except to say that they went to some great party."

I heard the doorbell ring downstairs. "Do you really want the details?"

"Why? Do you know something?"

"I know that Shane is happy and your mom is happy and you should try to be a little happy for them."

Noah groaned. "You sound like her."

"Great women think alike. I have to go. Avery's here."

"See you at school tomorrow."

A moment later, Avery waltzed into my room. "Okay, I have three possibilities," she announced, pushing the heap of wrinkled clothes off my bed and onto the floor. "You mind?" She knew I didn't. Avery laid out the three tops she had brought with her, each a different shade of dark blue.

With school starting the next day, Avery had volunteered

to come over and help me pick out clothes that wouldn't draw too much attention to my sling. I stood still while she held each of the blouses against my skin.

"Too light," she declared, tossing a crinkly peasant blouse to the side.

"This is why I need you," I said. "That was my first choice."

Avery appraised the pile on my bed. "We want something like you wore last night, but more casual. The darker, the better, I think." The corner of her mouth curled into a smile. "Although I have to say, Harris definitely wasn't paying attention to your cast last night."

"It's not a cast, it's a sling. And I think he felt sorry for me."

"So that was a pity kiss he gave you at midnight?"

I immediately looked down, embarrassed. I had no idea that Avery had witnessed the kiss. It had been so public, though. *Everyone* must have seen it.

"So?"

I looked up. "So what?"

"Was that a friendly peck or something more?"

"It was, you know, the whole midnight-on-New-Year's tradition."

Avery smiled knowingly. "Right. Tradition. Tell me this. Do you like him?"

I hesitated. I did like Harris, but I didn't know him at all. I liked that he was taller than me and had a great smile. I liked that he was nice and athletic and had a sense of humor. He seemed great—on paper. But I couldn't shake the feeling that he had chosen me, and, since I barely knew him, I couldn't figure out what it was that he liked about me. I was slightly suspicious. Was he genuinely interested in me or was he attracted more to his idea of me, whatever that was? More than once, someone had pretended to like me when in reality, all they wanted was a chance to be on TV for a couple seconds. When I expressed this to Avery, she frowned.

"Any chance you're over-thinking this?" she asked. "I mean, I've known Harris since kindergarten. He's a nice guy who wants to get to know you better. That's all."

Hearing her say that helped me relax. "You're probably right."

"Of course I'm right. He's one of the most—" She was startled quiet by the slamming of the front door downstairs. We both turned to look at my open door as heavy footsteps pounded up the stairs. Before they could reach the hallway, though, we heard my dad's voice.

"Fine! Avoid the question like you always do!"

The footsteps stopped as my mom turned around and went back downstairs. "I am not avoiding anything except yet another screaming match! If you calm down, maybe we can discuss this."

My parents were standing at the bottom of the stairs, completely oblivious to the fact that I was home and that Avery was over. I wasn't sure what to do, so I just stood there, hoping they would retreat to another room and lower their voices.

"We agreed that we no longer needed this kind of assistance." Dad spoke loud and fast, like he was trying to prevent Mom from interrupting. "And yet you keep going over there. We have a massive caseload and a full schedule, and you insist on wasting valuable time listening to some head cases with no degrees whatsoever fill your head with New Age nonsense!"

Mom kept her voice calm. "So if they had graduate degrees, you'd listen to their ideas? Their opinions would hold some value to you, is that what you're saying? I never thought you were that pompous, Patrick. I really didn't."

"Again, you're avoiding my original point!" Dad exploded.

"Which was?"

"Which was that we do not have time for psychic drivel. We have a reputation to uphold, Karen. I will not allow you to destroy over twenty years' worth of respected scientific research—"

Now Mom exploded. "You will not *allow* me? Is that what you said?" she screamed. "Since when do you *allow* me to do anything? I thought we were a team! Or does that only apply when I'm on board with what you want? Heaven forbid that I should have an opinion that diverges from yours—"

I'd had enough. I crossed my room and slammed the door shut. My parents immediately got quiet. I turned to Avery. "I'm really sorry you had to hear that."

She waved a hand. "Don't worry about it. I heard a lot worse when my parents were getting a divorce." Her eyes widened. "I don't mean—"

"No, it's all right." I returned to my bed and sat down next to her. "They're not usually like that. It's stress, I think. It'll blow over."

I wasn't sure if I was trying to convince Avery or myself. I felt like I was waiting for some defining moment when my parents would finally realize how stupid and pointless all their arguing had become. Then they would make up and everything would be back to the way it was, maybe even better. They just needed a little more time.

Avery held up the remaining two shirts and looked at them for a full minute before making a decision. "This one," she said, holding a silky midnight-blue top next to my sling. "Perfect color. Plus, it has a square neck, which looks great on anyone."

"Thanks, Avery." I knew I sounded less than thrilled, but I also knew she understood my shift in mood.

After Avery left, I tried calling Annalise. She had already

returned to Charleston. I knew that if she hadn't been dating Mills, she would have stayed home for a few more days. She might have even overheard our parents' most recent outburst. Then she would have finally understood how serious things were at home.

Annalise's phone rang once and went straight to voice mail. "It's me," I said. "Call me soon, okay?"

I wanted to talk to my big sister. I wanted her to reassure me that everything would be fine. I wanted her to give me advice about Harris and my senior year and college choices. We'd been so busy helping our parents with their investigation in Ohio that we hadn't really talked during the holidays. I felt like I'd wasted a chance.

There was a tap at my door. "Charlotte?"

"Come in."

Dad smiled nervously as he entered my room and looked around. "Hey, it's almost clean."

"Give me another day and I'll have it back to its normal messy state."

He pulled out my desk chair and turned it so he was facing me. I sat cross-legged on my bed and tried to keep my face blank. The last time Dad had visited my room was when he'd needed to set up equipment to monitor for potential paranormal activity. He followed a general rule of never coming into our rooms unless absolutely necessary. Annalise and I had always joked that he was worried he would glimpse our bras or something distinctly feminine.

Dad cleared his throat. "So, um, I guess you heard your mother and me downstairs earlier."

I looked at my hands. "It was hard not to."

"Right. Well, I want to apologize. If your mother and I had known that you and Avery were up here, we would have been more careful."

"You mean careful to fight more quietly?" I was surprised by how bitter I sounded, but Dad didn't look fazed at all.

"Your mother and I are going through a stressful time right now," he said. "It happens. We're working on it, though."

"Can you work faster?"

Dad gave me a tiny, tense smile. "We'll try." He pointed toward my arm sling. "How are you? Managing all right?"

I didn't like that he was changing the subject. I wanted him to promise me that everything was going to be fine, that their problems were all just one big misunderstanding. Instead, he was focused on my injury.

"I'll be fine. It only aches a little."

"Good. Try not to move it much. And don't worry—I haven't forgotten who's responsible. He's not going to get away with this, I promise."

"Dad, I honestly don't think Marcus meant to hurt me," I started. "I mean, he didn't—"

Dad held up a hand. "Enough. Let me handle this, Charlotte. You don't need to worry about it." He got up to leave, but before he reached the door, he paused. "We're conducting an investigation next month. You interested?"

"Sure."

Dad smiled. "That's my girl."

He left my room, and for a split second it almost felt like everything was back to normal.

Almost.

# six

When most people think of a demon, they probably picture a large, horned creature writhing in a fiery pit deep within the earth. Maybe they imagine a face composed of a cruel and twisted sneer with deep, swirled scars and blood-red eyes. Or perhaps they envision claws and teeth and the growling voice of a lumbering creature hungry for innocent souls. These are the features most people probably associate with demons.

Not me.

I was raised to believe that *demon* was simply a word given to a type of unique energy. My parents theorized that throughout history people had named the different forms of residual energy that the living left behind. For example, *ghosts* and *apparitions* were simply terms assigned to some things that couldn't yet be explained, occurrences such as phantom footsteps or disembodied voices.

A demon, they said, was a more intense form of residual energy. It was stronger than typical residual energy because it was not the result of repetition or anger or even grief. It was stronger because it was the remnant of something much worse: evil. People might not believe in the paranormal, but they didn't have to look much further than the local news to hear all kinds of true horror stories. Encountering real demonic energy was, thankfully, a rare experience. My parents took it seriously, and Annalise and I had never accompanied them to an investigation in which there had been any kind of documented violence. They knew how strong that energy could be and they did not want to risk exposing us to it.

So while both Mom and Dad believed that some residual energy could manifest itself in powerful ways, it was still simply energy, not an animated creature with a personality who set out to hurt specific people. It was something to be handled carefully, documented and studied, and then, possibly, diffused.

*Demon* was merely a word. But it was one I'd been thinking about a lot lately. It was on my mind as I carefully removed books from my locker before lunch, which may have explained why I was so preoccupied and lost my grip on my chemistry textbook. It hit the floor with a solid thud. "Great," I muttered. It was the first day back at school, and I'd had problems all morning as I'd tried to balance books with one arm. I was becoming more and more frustrated with the amount of time and effort it was taking me to get to class. As I bent down to pick it up, I lost hold of my English textbook. Before it could hit the floor, though, someone reached out and grabbed it.

I smiled at Harris. "Nice catch."

He held on to my books. "Yeah, well, it's good practice for me in the off-season."

"Catching books instead of catching footballs?"

Harris leaned against my locker. "Whatever works." He nodded toward my arm sling. "I was thinking about you. I thought you might need a little help today."

My mind was swirling. He had been thinking about me? He wanted to help me carry my books around? I felt tingly, but I didn't want him to see me as a feeble girl in need of rescuing. At the same time, I did need some assistance. My arm still ached when I put too much pressure on it, and a pile of heavy books would only make it worse.

"I guess I could use help," I admitted to him with a smile. I handed him the rest of my stuff and shut my locker. We began walking down the busy hallway. "This in no way means I'm helpless," I informed him.

"Of course not. It means that I feel guilty."

I looked at him. "Why would you feel guilty?"

"I dragged you to that party." We turned down the hall. "I should have known that wouldn't be something you'd like. I mean, you probably do stuff like that all the time, right?"

"Not exactly." I realized we were headed in the wrong direction. "I need to stop by the main office first," I explained. "They messed up my schedule. You mind?"

"Not at all. It gives me an excuse to be late to trigonometry."

The main office was packed with students, all of them grumbling about scheduling problems.

I eyed the long line. "Maybe I should come back later."

Harris wouldn't hear of it. "This way." He snaked his way past people, his hand firmly grasping mine. I didn't like to cut, but Harris plowed forward with such confidence that it was hard not to let him take the lead.

"I'm not here about my schedule," he announced to the secretary. "I just need to speak with Gwyn real quick." The secretary waved us toward a counter near the back. "She's an office assistant this semester," Harris explained.

I had been hoping to run into Gwyn. Our stories were connected, somehow, but she didn't know it yet. I wasn't sure how much I wanted to confide in a stranger, but I felt she would believe me. I didn't know how to approach her. Maybe, I thought, Harris could help me out.

Gwyn lit up when she saw Harris. "What can I do for you?" She leaned across the counter, forcing her chest up and creating sudden cleavage. I watched Harris's eyes. To his credit, he didn't even glance down.

"Actually, I need you to do something for Charlotte."

Gwyn's wide smile deflated and she stood up straight. "Oh."

I stepped forward and pushed my schedule across the counter. "Hi, Gwyn. I'm scheduled for economics this semester, but I took it last year at my old school," I said. "I want to drop the course and add a study hall instead."

Gwyn didn't even glance at my schedule. "Your guidance counselor needs to approve this."

"She approved it last semester. It just didn't go through."

"Yeah, well, you need to get her to sign off on the paperwork."

I felt my frustration beginning to surface again. Why did everything about today have to be so difficult? "I did all the paperwork. It should already be in the computer. And the guidance office is crazy right now."

Harris smiled at Gwyn. "I know if anyone can help us, it's you."

He was so blatantly kissing up to her that I expected Gwyn to laugh in his face. Instead, she leaned across the counter again, her eyes on Harris. "I might be able to do something. Of course, I don't have access to schedules or anything, but I can give you a pass to study hall and an excuse form for economics." She sounded unconcerned. "You still need to go to guidance, but this will give you a week extension."

"Sounds good," I mumbled.

"Sounds great," Harris said happily.

I stood off to the side while Gwyn printed out some forms and flirted with Harris. She obviously liked him and he obviously knew it. I wondered if he was like that with other girls. Did he use his looks and charm to get everything he wanted? Or did he have a history with Gwyn? At least now I knew why Gwyn was giving me a little attitude. She must have seen me with Harris at the party and hadn't liked it. I was actually relieved—it meant she wasn't judging me based on my family or what we were known for. But now I had to smooth things over somehow so she would talk to me.

For the rest of the day Harris helped me. As soon as the bell rang, he was waiting for me outside my classroom or near my locker.

"You should be careful," I told him. "I might get used to this."

"That wouldn't be a problem for me," he said. It was the end of the day and I was headed to my final—and favorite—class, AV, where I would edit the daily school news footage with Noah.

Harris smirked when we reached the AV room. "Couldn't get out of this one? Maybe I can talk to Gwyn again."

I was slightly annoyed. "I like this class."

"Well, I guess it's an easy A." He smiled at me. "No offense. I just didn't think that cool girls took AV."

"Well, they should," I snapped. "The industry needs more women behind the camera, not just in front of it." Harris looked taken aback by my little outburst. Even I was surprised by how sharp my voice had sounded. "Sorry. It's been a long day without painkillers."

Harris nodded. "I understand. I pulled a muscle once during a game and it hurt for a week. I was miserable."

In reality, my arm didn't hurt all that much. It was getting better every day, and I was optimistic that I would be free of my sling before the six-week mark in February that the E.R. doctor had predicted.

I told Harris I would see him later and made my way to the back of the room. Noah was already at the editing station, staring intently at a computer screen. I slid into my seat, feeling like I had returned home after a long absence. As incredibly lame as it sounded, this was where I was in my element. Everything about the classroom felt comfortable. I belonged here, surrounded by equipment I not only knew how to operate, but most of which I could fix, as well.

"What are we working on today?" I asked Noah.

He was frowning at the screen. "Not sure." He turned the monitor toward me. "This disc was already loaded into the computer when I got here. What does it look like to you?"

I watched the footage. The first thing I noticed was that the video had been shot in black-and-white. The second thing I noticed was that the camera was fixed on one spot, and that spot was the senior hallway of our school. "Is this from a security camera?"

"Yep. Keep watching."

The hallway, which was lined on both sides with lockers, was empty. The date stamped in the bottom right corner told me that the video had been taken today, just past midnight.

"What am I looking for?" I asked.

"You'll know when you see it."

After a minute, I noticed movement at the end of the hallway. At first, it was so slight I had to squint, but as it slowly moved across the screen it got bigger. It was a blurry white shape about the size of a small dog, and it glided across the floor in a straight line. Within seconds, it was out of the camera range.

I turned to Noah. "Show me again."

"I thought you'd say that." He typed at the keyboard and

the video went back to the beginning. "So," he said as he sat back, "what was Harris doing out in the hallway?"

"Walking me to class." I focused on the center of the screen, knowing that the wispy shape would soon appear.

"That was nice of him."

"Uh-huh." The shape was moving at the end of the hallway, against the back wall. It was very white and looked exactly like a dog, except for the fact that it was missing feet. A ghost dog? My debunker instincts were on high alert.

"So someone left this for us to find?"

"Yeah. It was right here." Noah patted the table. "What do you think?"

"I think it's staged." I froze the image on the screen. "It doesn't look like the stuff I normally see."

Noah moved his chair closer to mine so he could get a better look. "You mean because it's a dog?"

"Not exactly." I tried not to allow myself to be distracted by the light scent of Noah's cologne. I had a thing for guys who wore a slight musky aroma. I liked it so much that part of me wanted to nuzzle into his neck and breathe it in. The image made me blink hard. This was Noah, after all. We were friends, nothing more. Besides, Harris was sending strong signals that he wanted to spend more time with me and he smelled great, too. I banished all semiromantic thoughts from my mind and focused on the video.

"I would expect it to move differently. It seems to follow a straight line. A little too straight, you know?" I squinted at the screen. "I wish I could zoom in on it."

"Our school security system isn't that advanced," Noah said. "What I don't get, though, is why didn't the motion detectors go off? There's one at each of the main doors, and that's close to where this was shot."

"No clue," I murmured. "But it's got to be a hoax."

"A hoax set up when no one was around to witness it," Noah reminded me.

"Right. But the fact that someone slipped us this disc means someone wants us to see it, which probably means that someone staged it and wants an audience."

"But if it's fake, why send it to the one person in school with the ability to figure out that it's not real?"

Noah had a point. "I don't know," I admitted. "Let me take this home with me. Maybe Shane or my dad can figure it out."

He grunted. "Yeah, if Shane's not busy with my mom tonight."

I had to work hard to suppress a giggle. Noah glared at me. "It's not funny!"

I held up my hands in mock surrender. "I didn't say it was!"

"Wow. You two are working hard." Bliss Reynolds stood in front of our work station, hands on her hips. "I mean, it's not like we have a million things to cover for my broadcast tomorrow. Please, continue having a good time."

Whereas I was ready to lunge at Bliss for her sarcasm, Noah didn't let it faze him. "Hey, Bliss. We were actually about to give you a list of footage that was taped today. Why don't you decide what you'd like us to edit first?"

Noah handed her his notebook, where he'd scrawled the list. I was impressed—he must have come to class extra early or been stopping by throughout the day to see what had been turned in.

"Well, I guess we could start with the new vending machines," Bliss said, checking off an item in the notebook. "And I want to do a segment on Mrs. Demarse's new baby and the sub who's going to cover for her."

While Bliss was making her choices, one of her freshman

minions ran up behind her, lugging a digital video camera in his scrawny arms. I winced at the way he was manhandling the expensive equipment.

"Bliss! Guess what?"

"Don't talk to me until you've got at least a full minute of crowd shots that I can actually use."

"What if I got something even better?"

Bliss eyed him suspiciously. "Don't tease me, Matthew. I'm not in the mood."

"I thought her only mood was irritated," I whispered to Noah.

"Irritated is not a mood," he whispered back. "It's a state of mind."

Bliss and I had not started off the school year on the right foot. She originally thought I was trying to take over as senior anchor of the school news. After I convinced her that I preferred to work behind the camera and was not a threat to her dream of becoming the youngest female news anchor of all time, we reached a kind of truce. She was still pushy, crabby and wary of my motives, but she also recognized that I was good at what I did, which in turn made her look good.

Matthew was practically pulling Bliss to one of the computer stations. "You have to see this!"

My curiosity piqued, I followed them. So did Noah. Feeling him right behind me reminded me of the way he'd kept his hand placed on my lower back during the party. Again, I had to remind myself that we never had a romantic relationship. Besides, if his mom and Shane kept things going, Noah and I would essentially be family one day. We wouldn't be related by blood, but still. If things went wrong with us, it would be too awkward. It wasn't worth the risk.

Matthew was going through the video he loaded onto the monitor.

"Explain to me why you were filming the empty cafeteria when I clearly told you to tape the hallways in between classes," Bliss said.

"I did the hallway stuff earlier," Matthew explained. "I thought I'd get a few shots of those new vending machines."

Bliss was slightly placated. "Oh. Well, I guess that shows initiative."

"There! Do you see it? Right there!" Matthew paused the screen and was pointing to an object on the cafeteria floor.

"What is that?" Bliss asked. "It looks like a—"

Matthew hit a button and the object began to move slowly across the back wall of the cafeteria. "See? At first, I didn't even notice it. But it kept, you know, gliding."

It was exactly like the security tape, showing a transparent white dog moving without feet. A quick glance at Noah told me he was thinking the same thing I was: this was no coincidence.

Bliss frowned. "That's a poodle."

"A ghost poodle!" Matthew turned to me. "You know all about ghosts, right, Charlotte?" His excited voice was attracting looks from the other boys in the class.

"Shh," I warned him. "We don't know if it's real."

"But I was there. It *is* real. I saw it!" He seemed thrilled. "We have documentation of a ghost poodle. This is awesome!"

Bliss looked like she was trying to remember something. "The party." She turned to me and Noah, dropping her voice a little. "Didn't one of the guys tell a story about his grandmother's poodle? About how after it died, it came back to scratch him from under the table?"

"It was Harris," I said. "Harris told the story."

"Do you think that his story is somehow connected to this?" Noah asked.

"No." Bliss looked over her shoulder at the image on the

screen. "I think the story *is* this." She twisted a ring on her finger nervously. "Gwyn said freaky things would start happening after all one hundred candles had been lit. What if this is the beginning?"

"She said we would be joined by a hundred spirits," Noah said softly.

Matthew had already drawn quite a crowd around his workstation. Soon the entire school would know about the afternoon apparition in the cafeteria. I wished Avery was here. She had a knack for damage control, whereas I tended to freeze.

"We can't let this get out," I told Noah and Bliss. "Once this story starts, it's going to be impossible to rein it back in."

Most of the boys in class were absolutely giddy as they watched the video over and over again. Some of them had pulled out their phones and were texting.

"I think it's too late," Noah said. "The ghost has escaped."

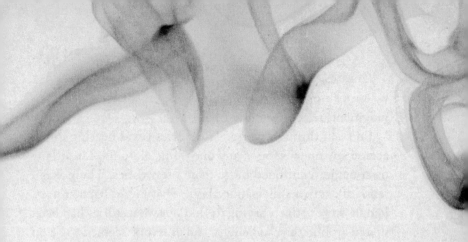

# seven

It didn't take long for news of the "ghost poodle" to spread throughout the school. The cafeteria footage was discovered Monday afternoon, and by Tuesday morning, everyone had seen a copy, thanks to the AV freshmen posting it on a blog and calling it the Demon Dog of Lincoln High. The video fueled rumors about the New Year's Eve party, which produced fantastic—and false—stories about what had happened during our peculiar game. The latest version involved more than fifty seniors wearing black cloaks, chanting in Latin and passing around a goblet filled with goat's blood. Harris, who had told the ghost dog story originally, was particularly offended.

"I've known some of these people my whole life," he said, referring to a group of classmates he'd overheard in the hallway. "I thought they knew me. Suddenly, they think I'm a devil-worshiping freak."

I understood how he felt, having spent most of my school years deflecting and defusing out-of-control rumors about myself and my family. It was never easy to be judged harshly by a misinformed jury of your peers, especially when their judgments felt so viciously final.

I'd been through worse. The stories I was hearing didn't accuse any one person of any one thing, although I heard my own name mentioned more than a few times. There was a sense of excited anticipation about what might happen next. People were actively trying to find out what stories had been shared around the candlelight, and everyone seemed to be on the lookout for continued weirdness. More than a few people had taken random pictures of the cafeteria corners and nearby stairwells with the hopes that they would catch an image of something. So far, they hadn't had any luck.

But the paranormal pandemonium had just begun, and I wondered if time would prove that the "demon dog" was a semi-isolated incident or the start of something really strange. Noah and I had kept the security-camera footage to ourselves. I had passed along a copy to Shane so he could debunk it, and I was hoping he would have a clear theory for me later in the day.

"Do you think this is connected to you?" I asked Harris, hoping he wasn't as easily convinced as everyone else. We had stopped in front of my history class before the bell rang.

Harris shook his head. "No way. Someone is playing a prank, I know it." His gaze wandered beyond the door, into the classroom. "Still, it's creepy. I saw the video, and it does remind me of my grandmother's dog. How could someone come up with something so accurate in so little time?"

I didn't have an answer for that. The security camera had captured the dog within twenty-four hours of Harris telling his story. If it was a projection—and I suspected it was—how could someone plan and implement it that quickly? They would need immediate access to equipment and video of a poodle. It didn't seem possible to pull it off so fast.

The bell rang, Harris handed me my books and that was that. The teacher was late, so the classroom was buzzing with conversation. I pretended to take notes while I eavesdropped on the people around me.

"Some freshman girl heard footsteps behind her in the hallway. When she turned around, no one was there."

"I heard the bathroom sinks in the east wing keep turning on by themselves."

"One of the seniors saw a shadow moving through the library."

None of these happenings sounded paranormal to me. It was a big school and footsteps echoed. Someone probably forgot to turn off the sink in the bathroom, and when somebody else entered, they saw that it was on and jumped to the conclusion that it had turned on by itself. A shadow in the library probably was a shadow—made by a person nearby.

As the excited conversations continued, I looked around and spotted Gwyn sitting a few rows over. She was hunched over her desk, scribbling in a red notebook. I wondered if she was having the same kind of rumor-control problems that Harris had mentioned. Everyone knew that the game had taken place at Gwyn's house, a house she claimed was haunted. She seemed to sense that I was staring at her, because she suddenly looked over in my direction. I smiled, hoping I appeared sympathetic. Gwyn frowned and went back to writing, this time moving her arm to shield her paper.

I really wanted to talk with Gwyn about the story she'd told on New Year's Eve. Had she heard the same voice I had heard in Ohio?

*Thank you for pushing back the curtain.*

It was an impossible coincidence.

The teacher walked into the room and ordered us to take out our books. I ripped a sheet of paper from my notebook and quickly scrawled a note. *Gwyn—can we talk later? Before end of day. Important.* Then I folded it, leaned over and flung it onto her desk. I watched as she unfolded the paper, then looked up at me, her expression puzzled.

*Please?* I mouthed.

She nodded yes.

Good, I thought. Maybe Gwyn had an idea about what this curtain was. Maybe the voice was not at all like the one I had heard. Maybe she had heard wrong, or embellished the story. I wanted a little clarity, something to convince me that our stories were actually totally different. Deep down, I was most afraid that this could be real. If a hundred spirits were going to invade the school, and if one of those spirits happened to be the same one that had spoken to Gwyn, then something bad was hurtling toward us. I felt my sling and the way it hugged my chest. It had taken only seconds for "the Watcher"—whatever it was—to inflict this kind of damage. I wanted to be prepared if it found me again.

While the teacher droned on about our next test, my mind wandered back to Harris. I was glad that he wasn't buying into the school's enthusiasm over the unexplained video clip. Too many people were accepting it as definitive proof of the paranormal, and it bothered me that a few seconds of footage had suddenly converted the entire school into staunch believers that Lincoln High was haunted. I hoped Shane would review the tape I'd given him. I'd asked Dad first, but he was swamped with a caseload that was growing by the hour.

"We're getting calls about everything from full-bodied apparitions to UFO sightings," he complained. "It's getting more and more difficult to weed out genuine cases of unexplained energy from the nut-job fantasies."

I told both my parents about the video and my skepticism, but I had been careful not to mention the hundred-candles game at Gwyn's house. Not only did I want to avoid their disappointment, but I was afraid they would use it as an excuse to fight, and I was determined not to be the cause of any more of their heated disagreements.

While my parents were determining their future cases, I was trying to determine my relationship with Harris. He still walked me to and from class each day, but I wondered if he would stop once my sling came off. Our New Year's kiss was as far as things had gone. Harris was not openly affectionate with me at school. He would sometimes put his arm around my shoulder or give me a light kiss on the cheek, but that was all. I was confused, so I turned to my best friend for advice.

"Do you think he really likes me?" I asked Avery after school. I had tried to track down Gwyn between classes and, later, in the parking lot, but I couldn't find her. Our dark discussion would have to wait a little longer.

Avery and I were sitting on the floor of her room going over our notes for a history test the next day. "He said he owed me for dragging me to that party, but it's more than that, right?"

She folded her notebook in half. "Of course Harris likes you. He follows you around everywhere."

"I know. But he hasn't asked me out or anything."

"We've only been back to school for a week. Give him some more time."

"I guess." I flipped through my own history notes, looking for the tiny stars I usually doodled next to something that indicated a potential test question. I couldn't concentrate, though. "What's the story with Gwyn?" I asked. "She seems to know him pretty well."

"We're not going to get much studying done, are we?" Avery asked with a smile.

"Sorry. I'm just trying to figure him out."

I didn't know why I was having so much trouble clarifying my feelings for Harris. Except for the hundred-candles fiasco, New Year's Eve had been great. Gazing at the stars with Harris had been, by far, the most romantic moment of my life. In fact, it had been the *only* romantic moment of my life.

Avery tapped her pen against her history book. "Harris and Gwyn's older brother are best friends," she said. "Greg graduated last year. I think Harris has known Gwyn forever, but she's his best friend's little sister, you know?"

"Who else has he dated?" I asked.

"Let's see. There was a girl his freshman year, but she moved out of state. He dated a couple girls sophomore year, but nothing serious as far as I know. I'm not sure about last year." She paused. "There was a rumor that he got busted at homecoming for making out with some girl in the parking lot."

This got my attention. "Wait. You mean this past homecoming? As in just a few months ago?"

Avery furrowed her brow. "I think it was him. I'm not sure. I've kind of been out of the loop lately." She shook her head. "Doesn't matter. Harris likes you, it's obvious. I say go for it."

Any questions I had about how Harris felt about me vanished on Friday. I had stopped by the office before second period to get my schedule straightened out once and for all. It was taking a while because one of the secretaries had lost her keys and apparently everyone had to stop what they were doing and join in the frantic search.

"I just need one thing changed on my schedule," I said. "I already cleared it through guidance. It will only take a minute."

"I put them right here," the secretary said. She patted the desk. "I know I did."

Gwyn emerged from the copy room with her arms wrapped

around a stack of papers. She stopped when she saw me, only for a second, then continued to her chair at the end of the counter. "Did you check the trash?" she asked out loud. "Maybe they got knocked in."

The secretary leaned over, rifled through the trash and smiled. "There they are!" She retrieved a big silver hoop laden with a hundred keys. "Thanks, Gwyn. I have no idea how that happened." She turned to me. "Now, what do you need?"

Finally, my schedule was fixed. I thought about trying to speak to Gwyn, but she was no longer at her seat behind the counter. I walked to study hall, relieved but annoyed that the process had taken so long, when I saw Harris. He was digging through his locker and didn't see me until I was right next to him.

"Overslept?" I joked.

He looked startled. "Charlotte!" His semishocked expression gave way to a smile. "I'm glad you found me."

"Have you been running?" His face was red and he was breathing fast.

"Yeah, kinda. I had to help my dad this morning." Harris's dad owned a landscaping company, and Harris was always running emergency deliveries for him. It seemed strange, though, that he'd have to do something for him on a school day.

He shut his locker. "Sorry I wasn't there this morning to help you out."

"I managed. You sure you're okay?" He seemed scattered, not at all his usual, composed self.

He took my good hand in his. "Better than okay. In fact, I wanted to ask you something. What are you doing next Saturday? Because I thought we could go out."

"Out where?" I cringed a little as soon as I said it, knowing I sounded stupid.

Harris laughed. "I don't know. Dinner, maybe a movie?"

I was thrilled. "That sounds great." I hoped I didn't sound overly enthusiastic. Harris helped me with my books while my thoughts swirled. Should I ask him what time, or would that seem too eager? I would need something to wear, but Avery would help me with that.

"Next Saturday, then," he said.

I could hardly wait.

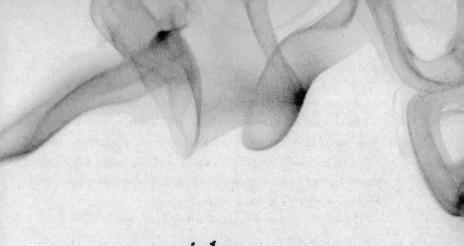

# eight

By the second week of February, I had successfully shed my sling, shared pizza with Harris on our first real date and definitively debunked the story of Lincoln High's demon dog. And while I was feeling pleased with myself, others did not share my sense of satisfaction.

After Harris asked me out, I was more anxious than ever to have my sling removed. I begged my parents to take me to see a doctor.

"You still have one week left," Dad pointed out.

"Six days," I corrected. "Please?"

Dad wanted to wait, but once I went to Mom and told her about my upcoming date, she relented. "We'll see what the doctor says," she told me. That was as good as a yes, in my mind. At my appointment the next day, I was practically bouncing in the waiting room, and when my name was called, I stumbled as I raced to meet the doctor, an older woman with blond hair and funky red glasses.

"You say this happened when you dropped a camera?" she asked, frowning at my medical records.

"We were up north for Christmas. I slipped on some ice."

The doctor removed the sling and slowly turned my arm. "Tell me if this hurts." It didn't, but having someone touch my arm, even if that person was a doctor, made me flinch. A memory of Marcus stung my mind. Those black eyes, that inhuman voice. *There is a price to be paid.*

"Do you feel safe at home?" the doctor asked.

I snapped out of it. "Yes!"

She placed my arm in my lap as if she was handling a piece of porcelain. "I don't mean to offend you, Charlotte, but I'm required to ask." She jotted something down in my chart. "Your injury isn't consistent with the story you told."

"It wasn't a story. It was the truth." I felt only a slight twinge of guilt for so blatantly lying.

After the doctor finished her examination, she concluded that my arm had healed enough that I no longer required the awful sling. "But no weight lifting for a while, okay?" She smiled at her own joke, but I knew she was still suspicious, something I told my mom about on the ride home.

"She was just doing her job," Mom assured me. "Really, I'd be concerned if she hadn't asked you anything."

"I know," I grumbled. The doctor's questions had felt intrusive. I wanted that miserable incident to be over, and the doctor's suspicions made me worry that there might be more follow-up.

Happily, I didn't have time to dwell on it. The sling was off, the weekend was approaching, and Avery had promised to come over for a little girl-time and pre-date preparation. Right before she came over, Shane called me into the living room.

"Thought you'd like to know more about your demon dog," he said.

I pulled a chair next to him so we were both facing the same monitor. "It's not my dog. What'd you find?"

"I had Trish take a look, as well," Shane said as he started playing the tape. "She's got a good eye. Watch this." He used a pencil to point to the corner of the screen. "See it?"

"No." I leaned closer. Shane rewound the tape and pointed again. This time, I saw a thin ray of light coming from the bottom corner. It reached all the way to the image of the white dog.

"What is that?"

"The light from a projector beam."

Just as I had first suspected. "So this is all a hoax."

"Yep." Shane paused the tape. "Which means someone went to your school after midnight, set up a projector—an old one at that—and shone the image onto the wall through the glass doors. They're lucky the school's security system is so ancient. If the picture had been clearer, it would be obvious."

"But it's just grainy enough that you can't tell right away," I murmured. "What about the cafeteria footage? Same thing?"

"Yep, although it's slightly more high tech. Someone could have set up a laptop instead of a projector, hidden it across the room somewhere."

"Like on top of a vending machine?"

"Sure. Case closed," Shane announced. "Now you can put an end to the rumors."

"Yeah, well, easier said than done." I was trying to figure out who would pull this kind of prank, especially one that played off Harris's story about his grandmother's dog. Something like this would take planning, and the incident had occurred the day after the party. The white poodle was not a coincidence. Someone wanted the school to believe that the stories told around the candles were coming true.

When Avery arrived, I told her about what Shane and Trish had discovered.

"So how do we convince the entire school it was all a prank?" I asked her as I sat on my bed. She was surveying my floor, which was dotted with lopsided mountains of clothes.

"I think a better question is, how do we convince you to actually use your closet?"

I pretended to pout. "I use my closet."

Avery held up a wrinkled shirt. "Not for clothes." She tossed the shirt in my direction and I caught it. "Looks like you're still using the floor system."

"It works, doesn't it?" I pointed to several piles near the bed. "Those are clean, those are dirty, and those are—" I paused. "Actually, I don't know what those are."

"Hand me your clean stuff. I'll fold."

Avery always insisted on picking up clothes when she was over, which I think was one of the subconscious reasons I liked having her in my room. She was a neat-freak, an obsession I both respected and marveled at. I knew hanging my skirts and folding my jeans wasn't the chore to her that it was to me. She had told me once that it was therapeutic for her to transform a messy space into a clean one. So really, I reasoned, I was helping her out.

"About the ghost dog," she began as she folded T-shirts into precise squares. "I'm glad you figured out it was a hoax, but I don't know if everyone at school is going to accept that."

"Why wouldn't they accept the truth?"

"Because they *like* the idea that the school is haunted. It's dramatic." She held up a red shirt. "This would be perfect for tomorrow, I think." She folded the shirt and handed it to me.

"Are you saying that I shouldn't tell people it was all made up?"

"Not at all. But I want you to be prepared when people

choose not to believe you. They'll say it's because your parents are debunkers, and so are you."

I smoothed out the red shirt. It would be great for my date with Harris, I thought, remembering how Annalise had once told me that I looked "long and lean" in it. "I don't know how much of a debunker I am anymore," I said. "I can't get over what happened in Charleston. It was real, I know it was. And if that was real, there have to be other things that are real, too, right?"

Avery came over and sat next to me on the bed. "Yeah. I saw the lights, too. I know it was real. But that doesn't mean everything is."

I wasn't talking about the lights, but that was okay. It was enough to know that we agreed, that we had both experienced something that night.

"Okay," I said. "Enough of that. Time for the real question. Which jeans should I wear?"

Avery plucked a pair of dark-wash jeans from my clean pile. "These. You want to look sleek for a Valentine's date."

"It's not a Valentine's date if we're getting together the day before Valentine's Day," I pointed out.

Avery shook her head. "But if the holiday falls on the weekend and you go out at any time during that weekend, it counts as a Valentine's date."

"Did I miss some secret meeting regarding the rules of dating?" I joked. Avery was an authority on all the things I was not, though. And at school on Friday, I had watched with more than a little jealousy as girls paraded through the hallways clutching bright flowers or plump teddy bears. Even Gwyn, who I'd never seen with a guy, was cradling an armful of red roses to each class.

I wasn't expecting anything, exactly, but part of me had hoped Harris might surprise me with something simple. I barely saw him at all during the day. My sling had come off on Thursday and he hadn't been around much on Friday. I worried that he had decided to no longer walk me to class, or was planning on breaking our date, but then he called me after school to explain that he'd been running errands all day for his dad. "He needs me right now," Harris said. "We're way behind on a major landscaping project. And why pay for extra help when you can make your son do it?"

I felt better. And my minor disappointment at not receiving a gift at school dissolved when Harris showed up for our date holding a single white rose tied with a red ribbon. "Happy Valentine's Day," he said. It was a sweet, simple gesture, and I loved it. I also loved the way he looked in a white button-down shirt and jeans. We looked good together, I thought, silently thanking Avery for her fashion sense.

Twenty minutes into our date we were sitting in a cozy booth at Giuseppe's, silently studying our menus. After chatting about school and teachers and people we both knew, we seemed to run out of things to say, and I wondered if Harris was feeling as uncomfortable about it as I was. I pretended to scan the menu, but I was really trying to think of something remotely interesting to talk about. When the waitress came to take our orders I panicked and forgot what I wanted, so I got the same thing as Harris, hoping he hadn't ordered anchovies.

"I haven't been here in a while," Harris said after the waitress had left. Now that we no longer had menus to read, we were left looking at each other. "It never changes, though. Always smells like garlic."

"Yeah. I love that smell."

There was another long pause. I couldn't understand why this was so difficult. Harris and I never had trouble talking to one another at school. Of course, we were always walking together somewhere and our conversations had never been forced to last more than the four minutes it took to get to class.

"So," I began in an effort to wipe away the awkwardness. "I think the demon dog has been debunked."

"Really?" He leaned forward, obviously interested. I described the light beam in the corner of the video and how someone just had to press an old projector against the glass door to make the dog appear.

"Pretty low-tech stuff," I said. "But I can't figure out why someone would want to make people think your story was coming true."

"Me neither." Harris tapped his fingers on the table. "I was talking to a friend the other day about the stories," he said. "I wanted to know about the things people were saying before we got there."

Now I leaned forward. "And?"

"Nothing too crazy. Strange shadows, footsteps, people hearing voices in empty rooms. But one story freaked everyone out, I guess."

It was one of the first ghost tales shared around the candles, but Harris didn't know who had told it. It took place in a gymnasium at another school, where legend had it that a freshman girl had choked to death at a basketball game. The crowd around her was watching the game so intensely that no one noticed the girl needed help until it was too late. She died in the bleachers with her hands clasped around her neck.

"That's horrible," I said.

Harris nodded. "So now people claim to see the ghost of a white-haired girl standing in the middle of the basketball court, trying to get someone's attention."

"White hair? Interesting detail."

"You don't believe it."

I couldn't tell whether or not Harris was let down by my lack of belief. "There's no real specifics except for the hair," I said. "It sounds to me like one of those urban legends that get passed around. Maybe it did happen—although I think a girl choked but probably didn't die—but it's too general to be authentic."

A guy approached our table and set down our meals. I was happy to discover that Harris had ordered meatball calzones. I immediately began cutting mine in half, then realized that the server was still standing next to our booth.

"Jared!"

"Hey, Charlotte." He nodded at Harris. "Hey."

"I didn't know you worked here." He was wearing a maroon apron over his jeans and T-shirt. A smudge of white flour was streaked across the front.

"I started a few weeks ago," Jared said. "I need to earn a little money for something I'm working on."

Adam's memorial, I thought. I didn't say it aloud, though, because I didn't know if it was public knowledge. We heard a faint buzzing sound, and Harris pulled out his cell phone. "My dad," he said after he looked at the screen. "I have to take this. Back in a minute."

Harris left to take his call outside and Jared slid into the booth. "I saw you guys come in. I was thinking about the last time you were here."

"I thought about that, too."

A group of us, including my mom, Shane, Avery, Noah and Jared, had come here to try and contact Adam's spirit. We weren't sure what happened, but our equipment showed crazy readings before going dead, suggesting that we had contacted something.

"Your mom was really great to me," Jared continued. "Shane, too. They helped me out a lot."

"I'm glad to hear it. So…" I hesitated. "Are you really planning a memorial?"

Jared smiled. "Yes. In fact, I want you to be the first person to see it."

I was surprised. "Me? Why not Avery?"

"I want your reaction first. Then maybe you can tell me what Avery will think."

Harris returned to the booth and Jared stood up. "Back to the ovens," he said. "See you guys later."

"Everything okay with your dad?" I asked Harris.

He looked out of sorts, like he was mulling over bad news. "Uh, yeah. It's just, he needs me back home soon. I'm sorry, I guess we have to cut our date short."

I should have felt more disappointed, but I didn't. We ate our calzones, talked a little more and then he drove me home. As we stood on my front porch, I had a flashback of Noah dropping me off after the Masquerade Ball, the way he had simply said good-night and left. But Harris stood very close to me, our noses almost touching, and pulled me in for a kiss.

"I'm sorry I have to go," he said softly. "I'll make it up to you."

"One more kiss and we'll call it even," I murmured back.

He placed his hand on the back of my head and pulled me in.

We were even.

# nine

Seventeen years of participating in paranormal investigations had taught me something that the average person probably didn't know: ghosts loved stairs. Forget the cemetery or cellar or creepy, dilapidated barn. Nine times out of ten, people reported seeing full-body apparitions on staircases. These apparitions either stood at the very top, sadly looking downward, or descended gracefully a single slow step at a time, or simply stood there, one pale hand resting on the banister. They were often dressed in Victorian clothes, for some reason, and were either translucent-white or bright green or shadowy dark.

"How many is this?" I asked Shane as I helped him unroll cable.

"What makes you think I've been keeping track?"

"Because you do stuff like that."

Shane laughed. "I guess." He made sure the cable was off to the side, against the wall so it wouldn't be conspicuous when we began filming. "I don't know about stairway spirits. Too many to count. At least a few every year."

I followed Shane back to his pile of equipment and helped him go through the checklist Dad had prepared earlier. We'd been setting up for two hours and were ahead of schedule. The drive west to the historic mansion had taken less time than we had anticipated, and we'd been able to get right in. The owner wasn't very talkative, just superstitious. She had inherited the property from a distant relative and heard enough local stories about it that she refused to live in the house until we could prove that she would be the only occupant. Dad was thrilled that someone actually wanted us to disprove ghosts rather than verify them. Of course, he used the term *ghosts* with a roll of his eyes. We often referred to energy that way simply because it was easier.

Shane checked an item off his list. "Almost done," he murmured. He looked over to the sitting room, where Mom and Dad were interviewing the fidgety owner. The property was one hundred and fifty years old and the original horse stable still stood in a backyard choked with kudzu.

"So how are things with the new boyfriend?" Shane asked.

"He's not my boyfriend, exactly," I mumbled. My love life was not a topic I wanted to talk about with Shane. He was too much like an uncle, and I doubted nieces had deep relationship discussions with their uncles.

"That's not what Noah says."

"You asked Noah about me?" I was mortified.

Shane shrugged. "It just came up. He said something about flowers?"

I knew exactly what he was referring to. After our abbreviated date the previous Saturday, Harris had mentioned that he would make it up to me. And he did.

On Tuesday, Mr. Morley had announced that I had a delivery. I looked up from my monitor, where Noah and I had been splicing footage for Wednesday's school news about new lab equipment. Standing inside the door was a girl holding a dozen dark red roses.

"These are for you," she said, thrusting the bouquet at me. "Is it your birthday?"

"No." I was completely surprised. Harris was sending me roses? It was official: we were definitely moving toward couple status.

I carried the roses back to my station, breathing in their rich scent as I walked. They were such a deep shade of red that they were almost black. Something about the color was exotic, way better than typical red roses surrounded by baby's breath.

"Is it your birthday or something?" Noah asked.

I laughed. "My birthday's in June." I sat down and searched for the card, but there wasn't one.

"Huh." Noah was staring at my flowers. "Looks like you got a baker's dozen."

"What?"

"There's thirteen roses there, not twelve."

I did a quick count and, sure enough, there were thirteen roses. "An extra rose? Lucky me."

"So you and Harris are a couple now, or what?" Noah's voice sounded funny, as if he was asking about a foul odor.

I fingered the silky soft petals of one of my roses. "We went out last weekend," I said, ignoring his tone. "We're not a couple, exactly."

"But you're headed that way."

Even though it was a statement and not a question, I answered him. "Maybe."

I set the roses aside and returned to my work. On the monitor, Bliss was pointing to new Bunsen burners. I barely heard her voice, though. I was too happy, too wrapped up in my flowers and Harris and that one word:

*Maybe.*

Later, Harris downplayed the bouquet, saying it wasn't a big deal. In fact, he seemed mystified that I was so happy about the delivery. He asked me out again, but I told him I couldn't because I'd already agreed to help my parents. For a split second I thought about weaseling out of the investigation, but I really wanted to go. I needed to see my parents at work together. I needed to know that things were going to return to normal, and that outweighed everything else. Including a date with Harris.

Four days later, the memory of the thirteen roses still brought a smile to my face, which of course Shane noticed.

"I won't pry," he said. "But tell me this. Does he treat you well?"

The roses were starting to wilt in their vase on my nightstand, but I didn't think I'd ever throw them away. "Yes," I told Shane. "He treats me very well. But please, don't talk to Noah about it, okay? It's awkward."

"Fair enough. I probably won't see him for a while, anyways. Your dad's keeping me busy editing the Zelden stuff and planning our next few projects." He shook his head. "The caseload is crazy right now. Your mom wants to hire an assistant to weed through the emails."

I'd heard Mom mention that to Dad. The brief conversation had stood out to me because they had gone from yelling to almost completely ignoring each other unless something was directly related to their work. I almost preferred the yelling. The loaded silence was harder to take.

"I wanted to run an idea by you," said Shane. "What would you think if Trish was our assistant? Would that be cool with you?"

I knelt on the floor next to him. "Well, yeah, I guess. Why are you asking me, though?"

He set aside his checklist and smiled. "Because, Charlotte, we haven't had a new member on the team in seventeen years." He winked. "You were the last one to join."

I felt a rush of affection for Shane. We may not have been

related by blood, but he was as much a family member to me as Annalise. I knew what he was really asking. He wanted Trish to become a permanent member of the Silver team.

"Are you sure?" I asked him. "Don't get me wrong, I really like her, but you've only been dating for a couple months."

"Which is why this is important to me." He shifted his weight. "If Trish and I have a real future, I need to know if she can be part of what I do, you know? Let's face it—this job is my life. It's a huge piece of who I am. If she can appreciate that and be a part of that, then I think we have a shot at forever." He blushed. "That was too much, I know."

I gave him a playful punch on the arm. "I'm happy for you, I really am."

"Thanks, kid."

It was nice to see Shane so giddy in love, but his happiness reminded me how different he and Trisha were when compared with my parents. I hoped that collaborating on a routine investigation together would remind them of how well they worked together and how, as Shane had put it, we were still a team. Of course, if Trisha ended up joining our team, it would mean seeing more of Noah, as well.

"You realize you still need to pass the scrutiny of Noah and his two older brothers," I said.

"I'm working on it. They're a tough crowd, though. Noah especially."

"He's very protective of his mom."

"Yeah, well, so am I."

The owner of the house emerged from the sitting room, clutching a tissue. "I can't sleep," she sniffed.

My parents followed her to the front door. "We'll do a thorough investigation," Dad promised. "We'll be here all weekend."

I looked up at this last statement. No one had said anything to me about spending the entire weekend in a moldy old mansion. I had given up plans with Harris for this. And if my parents thought I was going to spend the night somewhere without a change of clothes, my own pillow and a toothbrush, they were so, so wrong.

After the owner left, I went up to Dad. "What did you mean about staying here all weekend?"

Dad was checking his cell phone. "You know it takes at least forty-eight hours to do a decent job."

"No one told me we'd be here that long! I have homework to do."

Dad closed his phone. "I never said *you* were staying all weekend. Shane and I are conducting this one with help from a local paranormal group." He looked over me toward the front window. "They should be here any minute now."

"Well, how am I getting home?" Were my parents actually going to let me drive their car? I started to get excited.

Mom walked up behind me. "You're coming back with me. We'll leave in half an hour."

This was absolutely unheard of. My parents always worked together. One might film upstairs while one stayed downstairs, but never, ever had only one of them worked on a project without the other. Dad read the confusion in my face.

"Your mother did the interview, and we'll get some footage of her later," he said. "We don't expect to find anything, and we thought we'd give this local group a shot at it."

He walked away and I returned to Shane, who was pretending to study his completed checklist.

"You knew about this, didn't you?"

He folded his list. "Sorry, kid."

"How long is this going to last?"

"I wish I knew."

And I wished Annalise was with us. I had tried repeatedly to get ahold of her, but we were playing a perpetual game of phone tag, leaving quick voice-mail messages for one another at strange hours. I'd sent text messages, too, but I didn't know her class schedule, and even when we agreed on a time to talk, something always seemed to come up. It was aggravating. What was the point of having an amazing cell phone and access to state-of-the-art technology when you couldn't communicate with the one person you absolutely needed to speak with?

The local paranormal group arrived. They wore matching gray T-shirts and eager smiles and they gushed on and on about how honored they were to be working with the renowned Silver family. My parents acted like there was nothing wrong. Mom went so far as to kiss Dad's cheek, and Dad insisted on giving her a quick hug before she and I left for what Mom told everyone was a "mother-daughter shopping trip."

I was steaming mad when Mom and I got in the car to head home. I was irritated that I'd had to make the drive and spend my morning rolling out cables when I wasn't going to help with the investigation. I was angry that Shane knew more about what was going on in my family than I did. I was infuriated that my parents were acting completely phony and dragging out their little war rather than fixing the problem. And, as I stared out the car window and watched the landscape flash by, I was annoyed that Mom was driving in the wrong direction.

"We're supposed to be heading south," I informed her.

"No, we're not."

"Home is south."

"We're not going home yet." Mom merged right onto another state route, taking us even farther from where we were supposed to be. She didn't offer any more information, and I felt my anger grow.

"Okay, I give. Where are we going?"

Mom smiled. "Someplace where we can get answers."

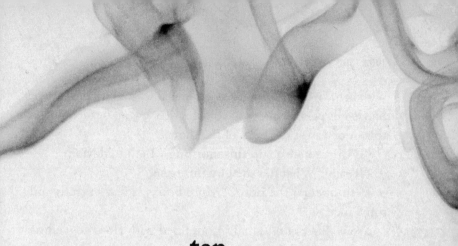

# ten

Apparently, Mom thought we could find answers through retail therapy. The tiny storefront she parked in front of was a clothing boutique called Potion, and from the outside it appeared to sell nothing but tie-dyed sundresses. The fact that the owners were displaying sundresses in the front windows during February seemed a little too optimistic to me. Or crazy. Or both. But when we walked inside, setting off a gentle tinkling of bells above the door, I realized that Potion was no ordinary dress shop.

"Karen!" A middle-aged woman with long auburn hair came up to us, her arms outstretched. She hugged my mom, then turned to me. "Charlotte, it's so wonderful to finally meet you." Her hazel eyes held mine as if she was searching for something, like she was trying to read me.

"Thanks." Obviously Mom had been here more than once. I figured this was the destination for so many of her mysterious "research" trips.

"Charlotte, this is Beth. She owns the store."

I half expected a more exotic name, like Esmerelda or Lady Topaz. Beth definitely had a New Age goddess thing going with her flowing green gown and metallic-gold ballet slippers. She led us past the racks of colorful dresses and beaded purses to a doorway at the back of the shop.

"Lisa was here again this morning," Beth told Mom.

"Really? What did she buy this time?"

Beth opened the door. "More books, a few crystals and some incense."

We walked into a small room lined with floor-to-ceiling bookshelves and low tables filled with all kinds of New Age stuff. The scent of smoky jasmine filled the space, and I spotted an incense holder smoldering in the corner. Whoever this Lisa person was, she had purchased her books and crystals and incense from this room.

"Charlotte, would you mind giving your mother and me just a few minutes?" Beth asked. I nodded and left the tiny room so they could continue to discuss Lisa and her shopping habits.

While I waited, I browsed the shop. Some of the dresses were too hippie-chick for my taste, but a rack of more formal gowns caught my eye. One, in particular, stood out to me. I pulled the deep orange dress from where it was hanging and fingered the delicate silk. It was a strapless gown with a tightly braided bodice and long, elegant skirt, which was draped in a light netting. I pressed the dress to my body and swirled once. It would be perfect for prom, I thought. The color was unique without being bizarre, and it held a simple kind of grace I loved. Plus, I realized when I checked the tag, it was my size.

"Charlotte?" Mom called from the back room. "We're ready for you, hon."

Ready for what? I thought as I placed the dress back on the rack and returned to Mom and Beth. They were sitting at a small round table in the center of the room. When I entered,

Mom stood up. "Sit here, hon," she said gently. She rarely called me hon. Something was up. I sat down across from Beth, who smiled serenely at me.

"I was telling your mother that I sensed something different about you the moment you walked through the door," Beth began. "I know about the incident in Ohio, but I'd like to hear your version of events, if that's all right with you."

I looked at my mom, who had perched atop one of the low side tables. "Go ahead, Charlotte," she said. "It's fine."

"Okay." I started with meeting Marcus and ended with the attack. Beth closed her eyes as I spoke and stayed so still that I thought for a second that she had drifted off to sleep. But when I finished talking, she immediately opened her eyes.

"It called itself the Watcher?" she asked.

"Yes."

"And it said you had pushed back the curtain too far?"

I nodded. "Several times."

"I see." Beth closed her eyes again. I glanced at Mom, who just smiled, so I kept my attention on Beth, who was now grimacing as if she was having a bad dream.

"The reference to the curtain is significant," Beth said, her eyes still shut. "There are people who believe there is a curtain which separates the world of the living from the world of the dead. Some theories suggest that there are times during the year when that curtain is thinner than at other times. Halloween, for example." She shifted in her chair. "The Watcher is suggesting that Charlotte witnessed something on the other side of that curtain, something she was not supposed to see." Beth opened her eyes and reached for my hands. I let her take them. "It has something to do with Charleston, I believe, something connected to what happened there in October."

"But we all saw the same thing," Mom said. "The Circle

of Seven witnessed the lights together. Why was Charlotte singled out by this thing?"

Because I saw a lot more than moving lights, I almost replied. But I didn't speak. I wanted to know if Beth truly possessed psychic ability or was just using information my mother had already revealed to concoct a credible story.

"Charlotte, your mother mentioned to me that you had clear dreams at that time. The way she described them, it sounded like you were having visions of the past. Is that accurate?"

"Yes."

Beth let go of my hands. "That may explain it. The dreams were not something the Watcher wanted her to see."

"Okay," I said slowly. "But what is this thing and why does it care about what I saw or didn't see?"

Mom pulled a battered red notebook from her bag. I recognized it as the one she often carried with her on investigations to take notes. "I've been researching this for a couple weeks now." She opened the notebook and skimmed through the pages. "Here. Read this."

*The Watcher is a term used to refer to an entity condemned to reside in between this life and the next. Thought to be a malicious guardian, references to the Watcher have been discovered in texts as far back as ancient Egypt, where people believed that if they stepped too far into another realm, the Watcher would inflict physical punishment, even death.*

"What I really want to know is if this Watcher is finished with me," I said. "Is it stuck in Ohio? Or should I expect an unfriendly visitor at my door soon?" I tried to laugh at this last part, but suddenly the idea didn't seem too funny.

Beth nodded. "A good question. I sense that, for the time being, this entity is confined, somehow." She stood up. "I have something that may help you."

"Help me with what? Why do I need help if this thing is confined?"

Beth placed a necklace on the table. It was a jagged purple crystal attached to a silver chain. "Just because it is confined now doesn't mean it won't find a way out," she said calmly. "It can't hurt to have extra spiritual protection."

I picked up the necklace. It was heavy in my hands, the thick chain spilling between my fingers. "It's amethyst," Beth said. "Wear it every day. The stone will eventually tune in to your own energy. If this Watcher finds you, the crystal should alert you."

I was now fully convinced that Beth was a charlatan trying to scare us into buying her jewelry. A simple stone was not going to protect me from demonic energy. I'd be better off hiring a bodyguard or getting a big dog or something. What I couldn't figure out was why Mom had faith in this woman. Maybe Dad was right. Maybe Mom *had* been brainwashed.

I looked down at the necklace. "How is this supposed to alert me?"

"It depends. Some people say the crystal gets warmer. Some say it vibrates slightly." She looked at the stone in my hands. "The stone not only tunes into your energy, but it absorbs some of it, as well. The more you wear it, the stronger it will become."

"Right." I tried not to sound sarcastic, but the idea of a necklace sucking up energy? I wasn't buying it.

Mom was still smiling as she came over to me and fastened the chain around my neck. "I'd like to show her outside, if that's all right, Beth."

"Of course. Just remember the rule." She winked and left the room.

"This way, Charlotte." Mom was pulling at one of the tall bookcases. It slowly swung back, revealing a narrow door.

"You've got to be kidding." We walked out of the dark room and into the cold, bright afternoon. I looked around me. "What is this?"

We were standing in what used to be an alley between Potion and the store next to it. The alley had been blocked off with brick walls, transforming it into an outdoor room. A room that had been renovated into an outdoor oasis. A stone bench sat in the middle of the space. White trellises had been mounted on each of the brick walls. Although it was still winter and most of the plants were nothing more than brown stalks, I could tell that this place was probably beautiful in the spring and summer. A pebbled path led to a fountain gurgling near the back.

"Beth calls it her secret garden." Mom said. She inspected a corner of the ground. "I planted iris bulbs here in November. They should bloom next spring."

She sat down on the bench and I sat next to her. "I don't get it," I said. "This place is so unlike you. Why do you come here?"

Mom stretched out her legs. "I come here because it feels right to me."

"Oh." A cold breeze rattled the slender trees. "Does this mean that science *doesn't* feel right to you anymore?"

Mom didn't give me a yes or no answer right away, but she seemed to consider her reply. After a minute, she began to speak. "Do you know how many investigations your father and I have conducted over the years?"

I had no clue. They had been actively researching different phenomena since before they were married, so their case files stretched over two decades.

"A couple thousand?" I ventured.

"My estimate is closer to four thousand."

"Wow."

"We've traveled all over the world. We've searched everything from national landmarks to ranch houses in the middle of nowhere. And most of the time, I think we've found proof of nothing more than overactive imaginations conjuring up very spooky stories." She folded her hands. "But we've also come across things that we simply cannot explain. Hundreds of incidents without any basis in science as we now understand it. Your dad believes that, with the right tools, he will one day find logical answers for everything."

"And you don't?"

"Charlotte, I'm beginning to believe that some things will never fall within the realm of science."

I didn't like that response. It made me nervous. My whole life I'd been told that you couldn't rely on your feelings alone. Just because you felt scared didn't mean you should be. Logic outweighed emotion every time. Now my mom was saying that might not be the case, that feelings mattered. It was like trying to solve a math equation with a poem. Some of what Mom said made sense to me. I had experienced something in Charleston, something real.

As I sat in the garden, grappling with my uncomfortable thoughts and fidgeting with my new necklace, Mom spoke up. "I forgot to tell you the rule."

"The rule?"

"Beth has one rule when you're visiting her garden—positive thoughts only. This is a happy place."

"Oh." I was fresh out of happy thoughts, though. I tried to enjoy the stone fountain murmuring in the corner and the bare, brittle stalks surrounding us, but my mind was tumbling with less than positive ideas. I gave up. "I'm kind of cold," I said. "Mind if I go inside?"

"Sure. I want to stay out here for a few more minutes, I think. See you inside."

I left Mom sitting on the bench, her face tilted toward the sun, a peaceful smile on her face. I wished I could be that tranquil. Instead, I felt tense, like I was waiting for something bad to happen.

Inside Potion, Beth was folding tunic tops. She looked up when I entered the main room. "Did you like the garden?"

"It's very nice." I looked around for a place to sit.

"There's a chair over there." She pointed to a velvet arm-chair near the racks of dresses.

"Thanks." I sat down, unsure of where to look or what to do. Music droned from the ceiling speakers. It sounded like wind chimes accompanied by a slow drumbeat. I found myself breathing in sync with the drums.

"It's great for meditation," Beth said. I startled a little, sur-prised to find her standing so close. "The music, I mean."

"Right."

Beth sat down on the floor and faced me. "It's okay to have secrets," she said. "I understand why you don't want to tell your mom about what you saw."

"What do you mean?" If Beth thought I was going to volunteer details about anything, she was wrong.

She cocked her head to one side. "There's something else around you," she said, ignoring my question. "There are people in your life who are not what they seem, people who are trying to get you to see things that aren't really there."

How specific, I thought sarcastically. Beth sighed. "I don't mind that you don't believe me. Skepticism comes with the territory. In fact, a dose of disbelief is a good thing."

"Sometimes we need more than a dose."

I didn't mean to sound harsh, and apparently Beth didn't interpret it that way. She just smiled her serene smile, then stood up and smoothed out her dress. "I'm very glad to have met you, Charlotte. I consider your mother to be a true friend.

And I want you to know that if you need anything, I'm here for you."

We heard a door open, and a moment later Mom emerged from the back room, looking happy and refreshed.

"I mean it," Beth told me. "If you ever need a safe haven, call me." She handed me a business card printed on heavy cream stationery embossed with golden swirls. It read, simply, Potion, with the store's number beneath it.

While Beth and my mom said good-bye, I puzzled over Beth's words. If I ever need a safe haven? What did that mean? Who spoke like that? I couldn't imagine myself calling her in the middle of the night and saying, "Hi, Beth, it's me. Got a safe haven?"

Mom and I were quiet on the ride home. I napped a little, lulled to sleep by the steady highway and the talk-radio station Mom insisted on listening to. Just voices, discussing local politics and sports teams and things of no importance to me. It was nice, I thought, after we pulled into our driveway and I woke up. Nice to be able to tune out the world and ignore the voices. I wished I could keep it that way.

# eleven

Avery needed a favor. "I want you to find out what Jared's up to," she announced as she drove us to school on Monday morning.

"What are you talking about?" I was more tired than usual, having been awakened in the middle of the night by the sound of my parents fighting. Again.

I had been too groggy to catch most of what they were saying, but I figured out it was about Mom taking me to Potion. I pulled my pillow around my ears and tried to drown out their voices. When I finally let go of the pillow, it was silent. Then I heard Mom, in a clear, sad voice.

"This isn't working."

Dad didn't immediately respond. I waited, and after a long time, he spoke.

"You're right. This isn't working."

I wished they were talking about the computers or other equipment, but I knew they weren't. I didn't hear their voices for the rest of the night. I didn't hear anything except the sound of my own soft crying.

When I dragged myself out of bed a few hours later, Mom

was asleep in her room and Dad was gone. He was always up extra early, but I knew something had changed. I could feel it. No matter what, I vowed, I was going to reach Annalise before the day was over. I sent her a text message after I got dressed, begging her to call me as soon as possible.

"Jared says he's planning something special for Adam's memorial," Avery said, pulling me out of my thoughts. "But he won't tell me what it is. I want you to talk to him during English class today, see if you can get a clue."

I had already told Avery about seeing Jared at Giuseppe's and how he was trying to earn money for whatever it was he was planning. The first anniversary of Adam's death was a month away, and Jared had been putting in extra hours at work. It had to be something big, but I had no idea what. "Why would Jared tell me anything?"

Avery turned onto the road leading to school. "Because he trusts you."

"Okay. So I should betray that trust and get him to reveal some secret that I then spill to you?"

"Someone woke up in a bad mood," Avery mumbled.

"Sorry." I shook my head. "I didn't get enough sleep last night."

"Really?" Avery smiled at me. "Up late talking to Harris?"

"I wish. No, just parental issues." I hadn't spoken to Harris all weekend, but he'd left me a few voice mails. I pulled my phone out. No message from Annalise. As we pulled into the senior parking lot, I turned off my cell and stashed it in my purse. I promised Avery I would try to squeeze some information out of Jared, then went directly to English class.

The room was empty and quiet. I slid into my desk and relaxed, letting my eyes close as I listened to the noise in the hallway. Lockers slammed shut, people laughed. It was a normal Monday. I was acutely aware of the jagged amethyst necklace resting against my collarbone. I was still getting used to the weight of it. So far, it hadn't done anything unusual, not that I was expecting it to. I didn't like it much, though. First, I had to wear a sling. Now I was wearing a fashion statement. Both had been pushed upon me.

"Rough night?"

I opened my eyes. Jared was sitting on my left. His normally shaggy brown hair was cut short, and his eyes held a clarity I hadn't seen in a while. Like he had actually been sleeping for once.

"Something like that." I watched him unzip his backpack and remove his books. "I'm supposed to ask you about the memorial."

He raised an eyebrow. "Supposed to?"

The first bell rang and people began to file into class. "Avery wants to know what's going on," I explained. "Maybe she can help. She doesn't want you to do it all alone."

"I'm not doing it alone."

"You're not?"

Jared tapped his pen on his desk. "Tell Avery not to worry. I'm doing something special, something she'll love. She should trust me."

The final bell rang and Doc Larsen rushed into the room, balancing a cup of coffee on top of a thick stack of books. "The computers are down," she said, sounding annoyed. The overhead lights flickered. "And apparently, there have been electrical problems all morning, so don't be surprised if the bell goes off or we lose power for a few minutes." She stared at us. "It's not the work of the fabled ghosts of Lincoln High, I assure you."

A few people snickered, including Gwyn, who was sitting to my right. Doc Larsen began her lecture about dead English poets and I struggled to keep my eyes open. It was a losing battle. I was hoping Annalise had left a message on my cell phone, which was tucked away in my purse. I slowly flipped through my textbook and propped my head up in one hand. My eyes felt heavy, and just as they were closing, something flew across my desk. I immediately sat up straighter and looked down, where a piece of notebook paper lay folded in half. I opened it.

*Still want to talk? Come to the office during seventh period. Gwyn.*

I nodded and slipped the paper into my folder. Then I tried to figure out what the teacher was talking about. I was too tired to hear much of what she was saying. The steady buzzing of the overhead lights was almost relaxing, and I felt my eyes growing heavy again. The lights flickered a little, then went out. For a couple seconds, we sat in complete darkness. Then the lights came back on, and everyone looked at the ceiling as if answers could be found there.

"Just an electrical glitch," Doc said. "Back to work."

She was writing on the board questions for us to answer, due at the end of class, when we heard it: the unmistakable ring of a phone coming from someone's bag. My first thought was that Annalise was trying to reach me. But it wasn't a familiar ring and I was sure I had switched off my phone.

We all looked at our teacher, who had stopped writing, her dry-erase marker in midair, and waited for her to start yelling about school rules and not having a phone in class.

Before Doc could pinpoint the source of the jolly ringing, though, another phone went off. And another. And then, within a few seconds, it sounded as if dozens of phones were ringing at the same time. It was so strange to hear all that me-chanical music playing at once that even Doc looked panicked. She must have thought what we were all thinking: something awful had happened, some national tragedy that was forcing our parents to immediately contact us.

She nodded. "Go ahead."

The entire class immediately reached down to pluck their cell phones from wherever they were being stowed. The music stopped when we flipped our phones open, but we could hear cell phones in other classrooms, all of them alerting their owners to the same thing. I opened my phone and checked the screen. Four little numbers stared back at me: 0413.

"Hello?" I heard nothing but static in reply, and a glance around the room told me that everyone else was getting the same thing.

"Is it a pin number?" someone asked.

"Looks like one of those satellite numbers. They come up as four digits."

"Mine says zero four one three."

Doc Larsen took control of the situation. "Obviously, there has been a technical malfunction," she said as she returned to the board. "I know that when I turn back around, I will not see a single electronic device exposed in my classroom."

Before I put my phone back in my purse, I checked the ringer. It was definitely off. I looked over at Gwyn, who gave me a puzzled look. "It's off," she whispered.

"Mine, too."

I could tell by the way people were examining their phones that this was the case with nearly everyone. It shouldn't have been possible for them to ring. And even if the ringers had been on, how could the same number dial them all at the exact same time? It was beyond weird.

I don't think anyone heard a word of the English lecture after that. Even our normally composed teacher looked rattled. I tried hard to think of something, anything, that could trigger all the phones at the same time. Nothing scientific or logical came to mind. I would talk to my Dad as soon as I got home from school, I decided. He would have a rational theory.

The bell rang and the class erupted into excited chattering about the cell phone incident. "Do you really think that was a technical glitch?" Jared asked me as we moved toward the door.

"I've never heard of a glitch like that," I admitted. "I'll ask my parents, though. They might have some ideas."

Harris was waiting for me outside the classroom. I no longer required his assistance, but he made a point to stop by at least once a day. I saw him right away, holding his phone and frowning at the screen.

"Did your phone go off during class?" he asked.

"Yep. Everyone's did."

Gwyn brushed past me, but Harris stopped her. "What about you? Did your phone go off?"

"Yes. And I have no idea what's going on." She gave him a hard look. "No idea."

The way Gwyn stressed the last part seemed odd to me. Harris looked confused. Then Gwyn walked past us and Harris smiled like nothing was wrong.

"We should get going," he said. "Don't want to be late."

"Sure." We didn't chat much as we walked to my next class. All around us, people were looking at their phones and talking about what had happened. Apparently, the entire school had been affected.

My next few classes were filled with a kind of nervous tension. Everyone was waiting for something else to happen, and rumors were already circulating about another demon dog sighting, phantom footsteps, and strange music coming from the gymnasium. And while people claimed to be creeped out, their smiles suggested that none of this was truly scary. It was like going to see a horror movie with a big group of friends: it was fun to be frightened, but when you were part of a large, noisy group, you knew nothing sinister was going to happen.

Finally, it was the last period of the day. I had AV, and I knew I would be able to get out of class for a while to see Gwyn and it wouldn't be a big deal. I ran into Noah as I headed down the hallway, and he walked in step with me.

"Think Morley will let Bliss cover the phone incident?" he asked.

"I doubt it. If he does, it will be short and sweet."

"Bliss was saying something last week about wanting to set up a camera in the gym. I guess there was another ghost sighting."

"Wonderful. I thought she wasn't buying into the hype."

"I don't think she is," Noah said as we entered the classroom. "But it makes a great lead story. She's always complaining that no one really watches the school news. A ghost sighting would definitely get everyone's attention."

We went to our computer station and Noah began looking over the checklist Bliss had left for him. While he did that, I pulled out my phone and was thrilled to see I had finally received a message from Annalise. "Hey!" she said in her voice-mail message. "I'm done with classes for the rest of the day, so call me when you get this."

Noah was still reading the checklist and warming up his computer and I didn't see Mr. Morley around yet, so I went ahead and dialed my sister. She picked up on the first ring.

"Hi, Charlotte. Sorry I haven't been in touch more. My course load this semester is crazy."

I skipped the hello and went right to the problem. "Mom and Dad are a mess and weird things are happening at school."

"Wow. Not the greeting I was expecting."

"I'm serious, Annalise. Everything's screwed up right now."

"Just a sec." She said something away from the phone. "Sorry. Mills is here."

"Of course."

She disregarded my bitter tone. "How can I help?"

"You can start by calling me back more often."

"Done. Now why don't you start at the beginning? Tell me what's going on."

Mr. Morley walked into the room. "Class meeting!" he announced.

"I have to go." I sighed.

"Charlotte, I want to talk with you, I really do. I'm going to call you tonight, okay?"

"Sure you will." I snapped my phone shut before Annalise could finish saying good-bye. Then I joined the rest of the class, including Noah and Bliss, at the front of the room. Mr. Morley sat on the edge of his desk.

"Lots going on around here," he said. "Some of you have complained that we're not covering the, uh, *happenings* in the school news." He looked at the two freshmen boys who started the demon dog website. "I had a meeting with Principal Carter. He thinks—and I agree—that this is all an elaborate prank. We've decided not to give the person doing this the satisfaction of seeing his work broadcast every morning. Extra attention will only encourage him."

"Or her," Bliss added.

Morley nodded. "Or her. Or them." He folded his hands. "After today's episode, though, I think I should warn you— this person is now in serious trouble. They have crossed a line and damaged school property. So if anyone knows who dismantled half the building's electrical system, it would be very wise of you to let me know."

The computers turned off with an audible sigh. "Not

again," Morley mumbled. "Let's see if we can get these up and running." He assigned tasks to the guys he knew were techno geeks. Everyone was occupied with something, so I turned to Noah. "Think you can manage without me for a few minutes?" I asked. "I need to run an errand."

"Go ahead. I doubt we'll get anything done today."

The main office was buzzing with a flurry of stressed-out secretaries trying to reboot their blank computers. I spotted Gwyn standing behind the attendance counter, reading a book.

"Hey," I said. "Is this a good time?"

She closed her book. "Sure. One sec." She told one of the secretaries that she needed to run to her locker, and I followed her into the hallway. We walked over to the vending machines outside the empty cafeteria.

"So you work in the office in the morning and at the end of the day also?"

Gwyn shrugged. "It was either that or take two electives I didn't need." She wasn't really looking at me. Instead, her eyes kept drifting over to the vending machines, like she was trying to decide if she wanted to buy a snack.

"Look, I'm sorry about being kind of cold to you."

"It's okay."

Gwyn was still staring at the vending machines. "Harris said I should try harder," she mumbled. She finally looked at me. "Is that what you wanted to talk about? Harris?"

"No! Not at all."

I wasn't sure how to ask Gwyn about the voice she had heard in her house. With everything that had happened over the past couple weeks at school, what would she think?

"This is awkward," I began, "but I really need to ask you something."

"I told everyone that this would happen," she said.

"What?"

Gwyn crossed her arms. "It took more time than you thought, right? But I said that weird things would begin happening after we lit all one hundred candles, and now they are."

"You know the ghost dog was a hoax, right?"

"So? There have been other things. The cell phones going off. How do you explain that?"

"I can't," I admitted. "Not yet, at least. But, Gwyn, that's not what I wanted to talk to you about." I pushed aside my confusion about why Gwyn seemed so hostile toward me and focused on the question I had been wanting to ask her for a month. "The voice you heard in your kitchen, the one that mentioned pushing back a curtain," I said. "What did it sound like?"

Gwyn looked surprised. "You want to know about the voice?"

I nodded. "Please."

She eyed me suspiciously. "It was distinctive." I could tell Gwyn was thinking about it, trying to choose her words carefully. "It wasn't a man or a woman's voice. It was neither. And both." She looked at me. "That makes no sense, I know."

I was already moving away from her. "No, it makes sense. Thanks, Gwyn."

"Wait!" She reached out for me, then stopped herself. "Did you hear it, too? In my kitchen?"

"No. I didn't hear anything in your kitchen."

"Then why do you want to know?"

"It's not important."

"What is wrong with you people?" she shouted. "Why won't you believe me?" Her voice echoed throughout the empty hall. A janitor peered at us from a nearby supply closet, probably wondering if he was witnessing the birth of a fight.

"I'm sorry, Gwyn. I didn't mean to bother you." I tried to keep my voice soft, but she was upset and not ready to let it go.

"Don't you get it, Charlotte?" Gwyn had lowered her voice, but not enough to placate the janitor, who was still eyeing us warily. "It's all connected. Everything that's happening here began at my house. There's something in my house, and things at school are only going to get worse unless you stop it."

"Me? How am I supposed to stop it? I'm not a psychic or an exorcist, Gwyn."

She glared at me. "Of course not. Because you don't believe in any of that, do you? Your superior intellect refuses to acknowledge anything beyond your power."

"My what?" She sounded like she was quoting something Zelden would have written.

"Forget it." She began to storm back toward the main office. I cast a helpless look at the janitor, but he shook his head and returned to his work.

I hated confrontation. I hated upsetting someone like that, so completely and unintentionally. As I walked back to class, I tried to make sense of some of the things Gwyn had said. She had said "you people," as if there was more than one of me and we had turned our backs on her. She wanted help and truly believed that something lived inside her house, something that destroyed furniture and caused her mother to move out. *It's all connected,* she had shouted. But I couldn't see how a fake ghost and broken kitchen cabinets were connected to one another, and as far as I knew, no one at the party had told a story about cell phones.

Back in AV class, the computers were still down. Morley

announced that we wouldn't have a newscast the next day. Bliss was upset, but everyone else seemed relieved.

"Everything okay?" Noah asked me.

"Sure." I wanted the day to be over. I was still exhausted from the night before and wanted to go to bed early.

"Really?" Noah asked. "You seem distracted."

"I've just had too many surprises for one day, I guess."

Unfortunately, I was in for a few more.

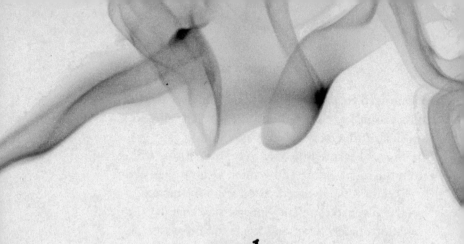

# twelve

It was the cookies that scared me. I'd experienced some terrifying things—a certain asylum immediately came to mind—but walking into the kitchen after school and seeing a plate of freshly baked cookies sitting on a plate, the chocolate chips glistening and melting, was enough to stop me in my tracks.

"Charlotte! You're home!" Mom emerged from the laundry room holding a basket of folded sheets. She set the basket down and went over to the table. "Sit down and tell me about your day."

It was a trap. Mom didn't bake. I wasn't sure she even knew how to turn on the oven. She was watching me, though, a wide, fake smile stretched across her face, so I sat down at the table.

She pushed the plate toward me. "Here. Have one. Have two!"

I picked up a cookie. "Who died?"

"Don't be ridiculous. No one died. Can't a mother make her daughter a batch of cookies?"

"Sure, a mother can. Just not my mother."

Mom frowned. "I knew the cookies were overkill."

"What's wrong? Tell me."

She took a deep breath and looked down at her hands. "Dad moved out."

I dropped my cookie. "He what?"

"It's only temporary," Mom said quickly. "He's going to be staying with Shane for a few weeks, just to get a little space."

"That's all? Are you sure?" I didn't like the sound of "a little space." Little spaces tended to become big spaces, which grew into wide chasms of nothing.

"I'm sure." But she didn't look at me when she said it.

"Well, if that's all," I said sarcastically. "Our family is falling apart, but a couple cookies and a few weeks' living apart should put it back together."

"Charlotte, stop. I know you're upset now, but this is for the best."

"Aren't you supposed to try counseling or something first?"

"It was our counselor who suggested this."

I could feel my jaw drop. Mom went on to tell me that she and Dad had been going to couple's therapy twice a week for more than a month. They attended sessions in the early afternoons, when I was at school. "We didn't want to worry you," she said. But I was past worry. It must be bad, I thought, if their own counselor was recommending a trial separation. And when had a separation led to anything but divorce? It was the beginning of the end, and I knew that the scent of fresh-baked cookies would forever remind me of that awful moment in the kitchen.

I retreated to my room. The thirteen roses Harris had sent me stood on my nightstand. A few of them were beginning to droop, their blooms bent over as if they were napping. They wouldn't last through the week. Not that it mattered.

I sat on my bed and pulled out my cell phone. Harris had already left two messages, but I didn't feel like talking to him. The only thing on my mind was what was going on with my parents, and I didn't feel comfortable enough yet with Harris to spill my guts about that. I took a chance and dialed Annalise, hoping she would answer.

"Hello?"

"Dad moved out. He and Mom got into this huge fight last night and he left. He's staying with Shane for a while."

"I know. Mom called me last week."

"Wait. What? It just happened."

Annalise sighed. "Yeah, but they've been talking about it for a while. They didn't have a date planned or anything. It's only temporary."

"Right. Temporary." I was livid. Everyone knew more about what was taking place in my own house than I did. Didn't I have a right to at least the same information as the rest of my family?

"They didn't want you to be concerned, Charlotte. They're trying to keep you out of it."

"Yeah, well, they didn't keep me out of their fights."

Annalise began to respond, but there was a crackling surge of static and then my phone went dead. "Hello?" It was useless—I was talking to dead air. My annoyance grew. I had just charged the phone—it was part of my Sunday-night ritual—so it should have had plenty of battery life. I marched downstairs so I could recharge it in the kitchen.

A little later, Mom went out for groceries. As soon as she left, Dad and Shane came over. While Shane worked on the computers set up in the living room, Dad gave me the same talk in the kitchen Mom had, using terms like *trial* and *temporary*. I nodded, knowing there was nothing I could say that would change their minds. Dad ended the conversation by patting me on the shoulder and telling me that things would work out.

"You'll see," he promised. "This is all for the best."

No, I thought. The best would be if you and Mom could settle your differences and we could all move on as one big, happy family. The best would be if none of this had ever happened. We are far, far away from what is best.

I stayed in the kitchen for a while and listened to the sound of Dad and Shane as they debated on footage for the next DVD. Later, Shane came into the room to get a drink and saw me sitting at the table, staring into space.

"Hey, kid," he said as he poured himself some iced tea. "Want to talk about it?"

"No," I replied. "I'm done talking about it. Or listening to it, for that matter."

Shane nodded. "Want to focus on something else instead?"

I was hopeful. "Like what?"

"Some tape from over the weekend. Nothing too exciting, but maybe you'll see something."

It was just the distraction I needed. Sitting down in front of a monitor felt so familiar, and having Dad and Shane there with me made it even better. Of course, the scenario would have been perfect if Mom were with us, but I pushed that out of my mind and focused on the night-vision footage in front of me, most of which featured the local group that had come to work with Dad.

"They're a little overeager," Dad said. "A few of them show promise, though."

After an hour of watching grown men panic every time the wood creaked beneath their feet, I was ready for a break. I was also ready to talk about the cell phone incident at school.

"Something happened today," I began. Dad and Shane leaned back in their chairs, as ready for a break as I was. "All of the cell phones within the school went off at the same time. What would cause that to happen?"

"Cell tower malfunction in the area?" Shane asked.

"That may affect certain phones, but all of them?" Dad turned to me. "Are you sure it was every one? Maybe the majority of phones were connected to the same provider."

"No, it was all of them. And the calls came from the same four-digit number."

"Satellite phone," Shane said. "Not sure how it could call everyone at once, though. How many phones are we talking about here?"

"There are five hundred in the student body. At least four hundred had phones, I would guess. And most of them were turned off."

"Not possible," Dad declared.

"Well, it happened. I was there." I got up to retrieve my phone from the kitchen. It was still charging, but I unhooked it and handed it to my dad. "Check the history."

As he was examining it, our home phone rang, so I returned to the kitchen.

"Hello?"

There was a pause. Then I heard a familiar male voice. "Karen? Karen Silver?"

"Dr. Zelden?"

Dad heard me from the other room and got up.

"Is this Charlotte?"

Dad was now standing in the kitchen doorway. "Give me the phone," he demanded. But Dr. Zelden sounded worried. Something was wrong.

"Yes, this is Charlotte. Is everything okay?"

"No, I'm afraid it is not. Charlotte, I need you to tell me if anything, um, *unusual* has been happening to you lately. It's very important."

"Why? What's going on?"

"Listen to me very carefully. I believe that you—"

Dad grabbed the phone from me before I could hear any more. "How dare you call my home!" he shouted into the receiver. "You are not to contact anyone in my family, especially not my daughters, do you understand? If you have anything to say, you can say it to my lawyer. He'll be in touch."

With that, Dad slammed down the phone, then stormed into the living room. "I want that man out of our lives," he fumed. "I've held back on legal action, but that's it. I'm done playing games."

Shane and I shared an anxious glance. Dad had never been so angry. He'd raised his voice more in the past two months than he had throughout my entire life. Everything set him off. It was like he'd grown a temper overnight.

"He sounded concerned," I said. *I need you to tell me if anything unusual has been happening to you.* Was Zelden connected to the cell phone malfunction? That was the only really unusual thing that had happened recently, and it hadn't happened only to me, but to the entire school. The demon dog was a hoax, and I was sure that the other things people were saying, such as hearing footsteps in the empty hallways and sinks turning on in the bathrooms, were nothing more than eager imaginations at work.

"Of course Zelden was concerned!" Dad put on his jacket. "He was checking to see how far I'd gone with the lawsuit. Your mother convinced me to back off, but now that he's called our home I'm going forward with it."

I wanted to remind him that at the moment, it wasn't his home at all. Dad gave me a quick, tight hug. "I will take care of this," he said. "You don't need to worry about anything."

Right. No need to worry about the fact that my parents weren't living in the same house, or that someone was trying to convince the entire student body that the school was haunted, or that Zelden was worried about unusual things happening to me.

I knew there were certain things Dad could take care of. It was everything else that had me scared.

# thirteen

"March madness" had taken on an entirely new level of meaning at school. It wasn't just that our basketball team was doing well or that spring break was getting closer or that the weather had settled into warm perfection, creating shades of green outside the cafeteria windows that made everyone inside ache to be outside. "March madness" was the term being tossed around the hallways to refer to all of the craziness that was erupting inside the school, beginning with an assortment of small, odd things that no one could explain.

Two weeks after the cell phone incident—something I still hadn't figured out—we arrived at school to find every locker in the freshman hallway open. All one hundred blue metal doors faced out. For a while, no one touched them, as if we were afraid they might be rigged with explosives. A few days later, we came in to discover every single chair in the cafeteria had been lined up, single file, against the wall leading to the gym. Throughout the week, the clocks would randomly speed up, the black hands circling all the way around several times before deciding to rest at noon, despite the actual time. Harris had been asking around and was trying to compile a list of the stories told at the party. So far, the incidents mostly fit with the same things described around the candles.

"Still think this is part of a hoax?" Noah asked me.

It was a Friday, and at least today, nothing unusual had happened, but everyone was on edge. Noah and I had just finished splicing together footage for Monday's school news broadcast, which featured Bliss interviewing seniors about their spring break travel plans.

"Of course it's a hoax," I said as I pulled up a new video. "So far, nothing has happened that a person couldn't pull off."

"Except for the cell phone thing."

"True," I admitted. "And it's the one thing we haven't been able to connect to a story told at the party. But it could still be the result of something we haven't figured out yet."

I knew I sounded like my dad. Even when faced with physical proof—like when our house was trashed by angry spirits a few months earlier—he refused to define it as anything other than energy gone wild. The only case that still bothered him was a brief encounter at an old prison with an unseen entity that had whispered, "Pardon me," as it had passed by him. That simple event, which had been captured on a thermal camera, was not something Dad could reconcile. But he tried, stubbornly returning to his research and tapes for a scientific explanation. I had a feeling he would never find the answer he wanted.

"Okay, so let's say a person is behind all of this," Noah said. He leaned back in his chair and stretched his arms behind his head. I loved it when he was thinking out loud—he took on a comfortable, casual approach as he sorted through his thoughts. "This person would need to be able to get inside the school after it was locked, turn off the security system and spend their time rearranging furniture, opening lockers and basically messing with things. Why? I mean, why carry on so many different pranks?" He ran a hand through his hair. "I feel like we're missing the message."

Matthew, the freshman who maintained the demon dog website, walked over to us. I was surprised to see him because he had ignored me ever since I'd told him that the ghost dog was a hoax. He had begged me not to tell anyone. "You have no idea what this website has done for me!" he pleaded. "I have a date. With a girl!" I told him that his love life was not my concern, but I did feel bad for him.

"I wanted to let you know that I have officially renamed my website," he announced. "Check it out. It's called the Haunted Hallways."

I smiled and nodded. I wasn't going to shatter his hopes again. If he wanted to believe the school was haunted, fine. As soon as he left, though, I turned to Noah. "Ten bucks says he's going to have to change the name again when this is all over."

"Yeah?" Noah opened up his browser and began typing in the web address.

"I'm thinking something along the lines of the Swindled Schoolhouse."

Noah smiled. "Nice use of the word *swindle*. You don't hear it much these days." He clicked on something. "Here it is. Take a look."

The Haunted Hallways web page featured the obligatory black background and spooky font. "I like how the headline drips blood," I said. "It adds a classy touch, don't you think?"

"The wailing ghost animation does it for me." He clicked on the photo gallery, which showed a still image of the demon dog in the cafeteria, although it resembled little more than a white blob near the floor. There were also photos from earlier in the week of the open lockers and the chairs lined up against the wall. More Coming Soon, the site promised.

"Lucky us," I murmured.

"My mom asks me every day if something new has happened at school, and she doesn't mean in my classes. She's really throwing herself into this new job."

"Yeah, I know what you—" I stopped and looked at Noah. "New job?"

"You know, as your parents' assistant? She started last week."

Shane had mentioned that Trisha might be "joining the team," but neither one of my parents had talked with me about it. They had never before hired someone without our whole family discussing it first. Annalise and I even helped them pore over résumés anytime we needed a temporary cameraman for a project. Hiring someone to work with us without giving me a heads-up was another depressing example of my not knowing what was going on in my own little world, and I hated that.

"Hey." Noah leaned forward. "What'd I do? You seem upset."

"It's not you." I touched the amethyst dangling from my neck. "I used to know what was going on in my life. Now, I have no clue what's happening in my own house."

Noah was one of the few people who knew that my parents were not living under the same roof. He'd been to Shane's several times, always at the insistence of his mom, and he'd seen—and spoken to—my dad.

"Is there anything I can do?"

I shook my head. "No. Thanks, though." I tried to smile. "I really like your mom. I'm sure she'll do great."

Now it was Noah's turn to look upset. He rubbed one hand behind his neck. "I'm not exactly happy about the situation," he said. "Shane's nice, but what if things don't work out with them? Her new dream job will become a nightmare. I think she's putting too much into it."

"What do you mean?"

"It's like she's rearranging her entire life for her boyfriend, and honestly, she's too old for that. I don't want to see her get hurt."

"It's sweet that you're looking out for her," I said. "But, Noah, did you ever think that this might be it? That she and Shane might, you know, go all the way?"

His eyes widened. "All the way? You mean, sex?"

I punched his arm. "Marriage! I'm talking about marriage!" I laughed at him, then realized how naïve he was being. Trisha had slept over at Shane's several times. What did Noah think they were doing? But if he wanted to pretend that nothing was really happening, I would play along.

"Well, once again class time turns into playtime for Charlotte and Noah." Bliss was standing in front of us, her eyes narrowed in a familiar glare. "Must be nice to not have to do any real work around here."

"Hey, Bliss." Noah straightened up. "We finished your spring break piece."

"Well, thank you, Noah, for actually doing your job. Would you like a medal? A trophy, perhaps?"

"What's your problem, Bliss?" I was used to her short temper, but she was being especially harsh today. "We finished our work. If you want to complain about us to Morley, go ahead. Otherwise, take your disc and leave us alone."

Bliss glared at me. "Right. I'll complain to Morley about his star student. That'll earn me bonus points." She snatched the disc from Noah's hand. "It must be driving you crazy that everyone thinks the school is haunted. For once, no one is listening to Charlotte Silver and her theories about energy.

Try not to let it bother you too much, okay?" She flashed a saccharine-sweet smile and stomped away.

"I think she's reached a new level in attitude," Noah said.

"A new stratosphere," I agreed. "Seriously, what's wrong with her?"

"I overheard her tell Morley that her grandfather is really sick." Noah reached for another disc. "Bliss and her mom live with him and take care of him, so maybe she's stressed about that. She shouldn't take it out on you, though."

"On us," I corrected him. "She doesn't like you because you hang out with me."

"We don't hang out," Noah murmured. "You have Harris."

Every time Harris was mentioned in conversation, Noah seemed to shut down. I usually ignored it, but now I wanted to know what, exactly, the problem was. "Why don't you like Harris?" I asked. "Did he do something to you?"

"No."

"Noah, please. What is it?"

He wouldn't look at me. "Forget it, okay? It's none of my business what you two do together."

"You're right. It isn't your business."

We worked in silence for the rest of the class period. When the bell rang, Noah put his hand on my arm. "I'm sorry," he said. "I don't have anything against your boyfriend. I promise. I just don't like talking about him. Still friends?"

I was relieved. "Of course we're still friends. And I'll try not to bring him up a lot, okay?" I wasn't sure why Noah was so bothered by Harris and me, especially since Noah was the one who had pulled away at homecoming. There was something about Harris he didn't like, but I had no idea what that could be.

After the final bell rang we left class together. Harris was waiting for me outside the door. He was driving me home because Avery had to stay after school for a prom committee meeting. She tried to get me to join, but I told her I was too disorganized and had no sense of color schemes. I promised her I'd go to the dance in May, though. I was hoping things would continue to go well with Harris, and he'd ask me to go. I'd never been to a prom, and it was one of my "normal life" goals.

Noah nodded at Harris and walked off in the opposite direction.

"What's with him?" Harris asked.

"Nothing." We headed toward my locker. "Actually, he's concerned about his mom," I said. "She just started a new job and she has a new boyfriend. Noah's afraid she might get burned."

"Why does he care?"

We weaved around the clusters of students filling the hallway. "He cares because she's his mom."

"Yeah, but, so what? If she gets burned, she gets burned. She's an adult. She can handle it."

We reached my locker. "I guess."

Harris didn't understand the situation fully. I didn't talk much about my family life, and so far, only Avery and Noah knew about my parents' separation. I didn't think it was something Harris would be interested in. Avery had been her usual supportive self when I told her, though. We were driving to school when I blurted it out.

"My dad moved out."

"I'm sorry. That's tough." Avery's parents had divorced when she was little. She lived with her mom and didn't have much of a relationship with her dad, who lived across the country with his new wife.

"They say it's only a temporary separation," I explained. "It's really not that big a deal."

Avery had nodded. "If you need anything, I'm here, okay?"

And I knew she was. And maybe Harris would be, too, if I gave him the chance. But somehow, it felt better knowing only two of my friends were aware of what was going on, like maybe the situation was still totally reversible, a crazy mistake that would be solved soon.

Harris and I reached the back doors when his phone buzzed. "My dad," he said after he checked the screen. He moved away from the noise of the hallway while I waited for him.

The hallways echoed with the sound of people slamming their lockers shut as they left for the day. I thought about the homework I had to get done, mentally organizing which papers I would tackle first.

Harris came up behind me. "Sorry about that," he said. "My dad needs me. I can drop you off at home, but I can't stay."

"No problem." I hadn't realized he was planning on staying at my house.

"You're the best." He planted a kiss on my cheek. "We'll go to the basketball game on Thursday night, okay?"

"Sure." He draped an arm over my shoulder and we walked to the parking lot.

"What are your plans for spring break?" he asked.

It was only two weeks away, but I'd barely thought about it. "No idea. You?"

We approached his car. "I'm going with my parents to the Isle of Palms. We have a condo there."

"Nice."

I heard my name and turned around, my hand still on the door handle. Noah was jogging toward us. "Missed my bus," he said. "Can I get a ride?"

I looked over at Harris, who nodded. "Sure. Hop in."

Noah got in the back of Harris's sleek black sports car. As soon as he started the car, heavy music blared from the speakers. Harris turned it down, but only slightly. "Where do you live?" he yelled over his shoulder.

"Just drop me off at Charlotte's house," Noah yelled back. "I'm meeting my mom there."

I saw Harris chuckle. He must have thought Noah was a mama's boy or something. It was a quick trip to my house. Noah got out first, but before I could open the car door, Harris pulled me in and kissed me. I felt myself sink into him, enjoying the sensation, but the kiss lasted a little too long for me, especially since Noah was standing right outside.

"I'll talk to you later," he whispered.

"Okay." I gathered up my things and got out. Noah didn't say anything, and I was embarrassed knowing that he had witnessed the most intense kiss Harris and I had shared in a while.

Inside my house, Mom and Trisha were at one of the computers in the living room.

"Tell Lisa I'll try to stop by next week," Mom said as Trisha typed.

"She says there's more activity at night. Do you want to visit her in the evening?"

Mom shook her head. "No. If there's activity at night, then it's also present during the day. It doesn't matter what time I go." She looked up as Noah and I entered the room. "Hi, guys! How was school?"

"Fine," I said.

Trisha beamed at Noah. "How'd the history test go?"

"Good."

"Why don't you get something to eat from the kitchen?" Mom suggested. "We're just answering some emails."

I led Noah into the kitchen. "Listen," he said. "I have something for you. It's the reason I missed my bus, actually." He unzipped his backpack and pulled out a disc. "This was waiting for me in my locker after school." He pushed the disc toward me and I picked it up. It was a normal recordable DVD, but there was a yellow Post-it note stuck to the front.

I didn't recognize the scraggly writing on the note, but I did recognize the message, and it triggered an echo of pain in my arm.

*The curtain has been pushed back again.*

# fourteen

The crowd of people above me were stomping their feet so hard I was sure the bleachers would come crashing down on my head at any moment. I hunched down lower and scanned the ground.

"What are we looking for, exactly?" I asked Noah. He didn't hear me over the suddenly jubilant screams, which I interpreted to mean that our team had scored a basket.

"Over here!" he yelled. I made my way over to him, carefully avoiding the sticky puddles of soda pop smeared across the gym floor. Every time I bent over, my amethyst necklace banged against my chest. I hated wearing it, but Mom was insistent. Whenever I left the house, her eyes scanned my neck to make sure the chain was secured there.

"It's really gross under here," I said. "Have you looked up? Some of that gum stuck under the seats is probably older than we are."

Noah pointed down. "See that?"

"It's a scuff mark from somebody's shoe." I frowned. "Noah, there are a ton of these on the floor. It doesn't mean anything."

"But this would be about the location of the camera. So maybe it belongs to the person behind it."

"And maybe it's just a random mark like the hundreds of others."

It had been a week since Noah showed me the DVD left in his locker. We had waited until our moms left the house to run an errand—I suspected Mom was taking Trisha to Potion and would be gone for a while—then watched the shaky footage together.

The first shot showed our school's empty gymnasium. The only light source was the red glow of the exit signs, so it was dim. The camera moved, and it was apparent from the motion that someone was setting it on the gym floor so that it pointed toward the center of the room. After a few seconds, the camera shifted again, this time facing a wall, and when it was moved back to its original spot, there was a girl standing in the middle of the gym.

A girl with white hair.

"This is one of the stories," I told Noah.

"You sure?"

"Yes. A girl choked to death at a basketball game. That's her."

The girl appeared on-screen for less than two seconds before the camera moved again, then cut to black completely. We froze the image, trying to make sense of what we were seeing. It looked like a real, live girl, not a wispy apparition. Her head was down, and the long white hair concealed her face. She was dressed in jeans and a gauzy white shirt, but strangely, she was barefoot.

"This is creepy," Noah said.

"This is another hoax," I replied.

Noah agreed with me, but I knew the image was unsettling to him. We decided to wait for someone else to leak it to the rest of the school. I was convinced it would show up on the Haunted Hallways website within a day or two, but a week passed with no mention of it anywhere. In fact, nothing at all unusual had been happening at school.

Until Friday morning.

Noah was waiting for me by my locker when I got to school, his face anxious. I braced myself for an onslaught of complaints about Shane, who had taken Trisha out to dinner the night before.

"Do you smell it?" Noah asked.

"Smell what?" I dropped my backpack to the floor and began twirling my locker combination. As I popped open the metal door, I caught a whiff of something fruity, like a very sweet perfume. I looked at Noah. "Peaches."

He ran a hand through his hair. "It's even stronger in the junior hallway, especially right near my locker."

"The story about your neighbor who died," I said. "This is it."

"I should never have told that story," Noah said. "It was way too personal. But it was either that or tell everyone about what happened to us in Charleston, and I knew you wouldn't want that." He looked around as if afraid someone might be listening. "If this is all a hoax, then someone is trying really hard to get our attention."

I agreed. And after the peach incident—which everyone detected and caused a fresh new wave of interest in the hundred candles game—Noah decided that we needed to discover, once and for all, who was behind the pranks. But he didn't say *pranks*. Instead, he referred to it as the *happenings*. I wasn't sure if he thought the cause of everything was human or not, but either way, he was now determined to figure it out, and figuring it out began with a trip beneath the bleachers, where we were sure the DVD of the white-haired girl had been filmed.

The footage of the girl didn't scare me, but the note attached to the disc did. *The curtain has been pushed back again.* As I read those words, I could almost hear the voice that had erupted from Marcus, and it gave me the chills. If someone wanted my attention, they had it, but not in a good way. When I found out who had been messing with me and disturbing Noah, I was going to expose them as publicly as possible.

After a few more minutes of crouching beneath the bleachers searching for clues that probably didn't exist, I tapped Noah on the arm. He turned around as a buzzer went off, and I had to cover my ears. "I'm getting out of here," I shouted. "Harris will wonder where I've been!"

Noah nodded and I scuttled out from beneath the bleachers. I glanced around, hoping no one had seen me. Luckily, most people appeared to be focused on the game. I wiped dust off my jeans, trusted that nothing disgusting had somehow fallen into my hair, and returned to Harris, who was sitting on the opposite side of the basketball court. We were supposed to be on a date, but so far, I'd spent half the time away from him.

I sat down and he handed me a paper cup filled with luke-warm soda. "You missed a great shot right at the buzzer," he said.

"Are we winning?"

Harris laughed. "Only by a dozen points."

Across the gym, Noah darted beneath the bleachers. At the end of the third quarter, he emerged with something in his hand. I watched as he searched the crowd. When his eyes found mine, he nodded.

The game ended. Our team won, which thrilled Harris. He was in a particularly good mood as he reached for my hand, giving it a squeeze as we left the crowded gym. Someone brushed past us, bumping me into Harris. It was Gwyn, and she seemed to be in a hurry.

"What's with her?" I asked.

Harris sighed. "It's my fault. We got into a fight right before the game."

"You got into a fight with Gwyn? Over what?"

"Over who," he corrected.

We walked outside into the cool night air and headed toward his car. It was just after ten, and I had a full two hours before I needed to be home. I waited for Harris to say more about Gwyn, but he didn't immediately offer anything. Their relationship puzzled me. Avery had said that Harris and Gwyn's older brother were best friends, and they'd grown up across the street from one another, so I imagined he knew Gwyn pretty well. But anytime they crossed paths at school, he seemed distant and she acted like she was bordering on the furious. It was possible, I thought, that Gwyn harbored a crush on my boyfriend, but I knew he didn't return her feelings. He barely acknowledged her. Maybe that was the problem. Maybe she wanted a piece of the daily attention he was giving to me.

We got into Harris's car. "You want to go somewhere? I'll tell you all about it."

"I'm up for anything," I said.

A few minutes later we pulled into a popular burger place, the kind where you can order from your car and stay parked while you eat. Harris ordered milkshakes and onion rings. "How retro," I joked.

"I love this place," Harris said. "There's more grease than meat on the burgers."

After our food arrived, I asked him about his fight with Gwyn. He chewed on an onion ring before he answered me.

"So, Gwyn and I have known each other for, like, ever,"

he began. "I was always over at their house, and she always tagged along with me and Greg."

"Her brother," I said.

"Right. Well, Greg left for college last year, and things between Gwyn and me changed. We don't talk to each other at school as much, that kind of thing."

I sipped my chocolate shake, relishing the cold, sugary creaminess of it. The drive-in's orange lights glowed above us, but inside the car it was darker, almost as if we were sitting by candlelight. For a moment, I thought that this could actually be romantic—if we weren't talking about an angry girl.

"I got to the game early tonight," Harris continued. "Gwyn wanted to talk to me about the stuff going on at her house. She says it's gotten worse, and she wanted me to talk to her brother about coming home from college to help out. I said no."

"What does she think her brother can do to help?"

Harris nodded. "Exactly! Why drag him here? Their mom is going nuts trying to make it stop. She's talking to witches and hiring all kinds of weird specialists to come in and burn grass or something."

I laughed. "They're burning sage. It's an old ritual called smudging."

"Does it work?"

I shrugged. "It makes people feel better."

Lots of strange things made people feel more in control, and the older or more peculiar the practice, the better. Smudging was a very simple, very common rite that I had witnessed dozens of times. The only thing it really did was make a room smell rich and earthy.

Harris played with the straw poking out of his shake. "This whole thing at Gwyn's house—it's got her really upset. She called me a few weeks ago, hysterical. She said a table had moved by itself."

"Sounds like something my parents might be interested in investigating."

Harris sighed. "Yeah, well, they weren't. Gwyn's mom called them months ago."

"Oh." I knew my parents were overwhelmed with the number of people contacting them, and they were doing their best to investigate the most serious claims. "I could talk to them," I offered. "Maybe Gwyn's case was overlooked, for some reason."

The smile on Harris's face made my stomach warm. "You would do that? Really? Charlotte, I can't thank you enough."

He set down his shake, brushed some crumbs from his jeans, and moved closer to me. I tried to move closer, too, but it was difficult with the console dividing our seats. Harris reached one arm over and let his hand rest on the back of my neck.

"I really like you," he said, his voice barely above a whisper. "I hope you know that."

"I like you, too."

"I know I haven't been as…*attentive* as I could be, and I'm sorry about that."

"It's okay." Our noses were nearly touching, and his lips were so close to mine that when I spoke, mine brushed lightly against his. "I know you need to help out your dad. And you've been great, really. Those roses you sent me were beautiful."

"The roses," he repeated. Then he pulled me in and we were kissing. His mouth felt warm and tasted faintly like onions and chocolate, but it wasn't a bad combination. Different, yes, but not bad. He pulled away first, but kept his face close to mine.

"I know this is early, but I want to ask you something."

I felt tingly from our kiss. "Ask me anything."

"Will you go to the prom with me?"

Instead of answering, I kissed him again. "I'll take that as a yes," he murmured.

After more kissing, we finished our shakes and Harris drove me home. The downstairs lights were on as we pulled into the driveway. "Looks like your folks are waiting up for you," Harris said.

"Just my mom."

I still had some time before curfew, and I wanted Harris to keep driving somewhere, anywhere, so we could be alone together and I could tell him all about my parental problems. I didn't get to ask him, though. His phone buzzed and he sighed.

"Probably my dad," he said. "Sorry."

I kissed him on the cheek. "Not a problem. See you later."

"I'll call you." He waited until I had reached the front porch before driving away. I watched the lights from his car become smaller and smaller until he turned down the end of the street and was gone. Then I opened the front door—and walked right into a disaster.

"You've gone too far this time, Karen!" Dad shouted.

Mom was more controlled. "Please don't scream at me, Patrick. It's not helpful."

I stood in the foyer, my hand frozen on the doorknob. My parents were in the dining room, and they would see me as soon as I shut the door and walked toward the staircase. I remained still and hoped to make sense of what they were fighting about this time.

"I have asked you repeatedly not to pursue this case," Dad said, his voice lower. He was still seething with rage, though. "And now you have not only done that, but you have chosen to bring *him* into it, despite my clear—and totally justified—disapproval."

"I understand that you're upset right now," Mom said. "But this was my choice to make, and I felt he could be very helpful to us."

Dad erupted again. "This was *not* your choice to make!"

I'd never heard him yell that loudly. It startled me so badly that I let go of the doorknob and bumped against it, causing the door to slam shut.

"Charlotte? Is that you?" Mom asked.

I took a tentative step toward the dining room. "Yeah. I just got home." I looked at my parents. They were standing at opposite ends of the room. "Hi, Dad. What are you doing here?" I acted like I hadn't just heard him scream at Mom.

Dad cleared his throat. "I stopped by to pick up some case files," he said. "I was about to leave, actually. How was the dance?"

"I was at a basketball game."

"Right. The game. How did that go?"

"We won."

"Excellent. Well, I need to get back." He nodded at Mom. "I'll speak with you later." He walked swiftly to the foyer, where he planted a quick kiss on the top of my head. "See you soon."

He left. Mom stood in the dining room, looking stunned. I dropped my purse on the foyer table and went to her. "Mom? Are you okay?"

She nodded, but I could see tears forming in her eyes. "Your father is under a lot of stress right now," she said softly. "I'm very tired. Maybe tomorrow you could tell me about your date?"

"Sure. Okay."

Mom gave me a small smile and went upstairs. I remained

in the dining room, wondering what had just happened. Why was Dad so angry about a case? And who had Mom brought into it? A man, obviously, but who? Maybe she had an old boyfriend she'd turned to? Or worse, someone she was having an affair with? But that didn't seem possible. Mom would never cheat on Dad. Of course, I never thought they would be living apart from one another, either.

My wonderful day, which moments earlier had felt so perfect as I kissed Harris, had dissolved into yet another bad memory for me. I wouldn't remember the night as the one in which I was asked to prom for the first time. Instead, it would be etched in my mind as the night my parents' marriage completely collapsed.

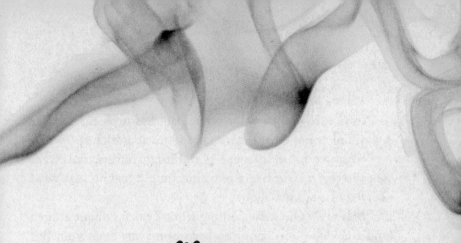

# fifteen

"Time is against you."

I awoke the following Wednesday in a state of confusion, Marcus's threat lingering in my mind. It was barely light out. I groped for my alarm clock, then frowned when I read the numbers: 5:49. Way too early. I plopped back onto my pillows, but I knew I wouldn't be able to return to sleep. Then I heard the sound that had roused me from my much-needed rest: the buzzing of my cell phone. I reached across my nightstand for it, nearly knocking over the vase holding my now-wilted roses from Harris. The phone buzzed again and I flipped it open to reveal an unfamiliar number.

"Hello?"

"Charlotte?"

I sat up and pushed the tousled hair out of my face. "Dr. Zelden?"

"I'm sorry to call you at this hour, but it was the only chance I had to reach you. I'll be brief."

There was a lot of static on the other end, and Zelden himself sounded like he was talking in a cave. His frantic voice echoed.

"Where are you?" I asked.

"I can't tell you that, I'm afraid. But I assure you, I am far away. I'm doing what I can to keep him at a distance."

"Keep who at a distance?" Confusing conversations were not the best way to begin one's morning. I had no idea what Zelden was talking about.

"Marcus." The static coming from Zelden's phone surged and crackled. "I'm trying to keep him away from you. But Charlotte, he knows where you go to school. It was on your sweatshirt that day at the asylum."

"I don't understand," I said. "What's going on?"

Zelden's voice was being swallowed up by the increasing static. "It keeps happening," he shouted, desperate urgency in his voice. "I cannot contain it! Watch for the signs, Charlotte, and find a safe—"

The line went dead. I kept the phone pressed to my ear, hoping that somehow, Zelden would get through and utter a few more words to clarify his rambling warning. He had sounded truly upset. Afraid that I would forget everything Zelden had said, I got out of bed and grabbed a sheet of paper and a pen.

*He's trying to keep Marcus far away from me.*

*Marcus knows where I go to school.*

*Something keeps happening and can't be contained.*

*I need to look out for signs and find safety.*

But he hadn't said *safety,* I realized as I came to the end of my little list. He had been cut off. I remembered Beth from Potion. She had told me that if I ever needed a safe haven, I should call her. Was that what Zelden was about to say? *Find a safe haven.* It was an odd word and an even odder request.

Beth had also said the Watcher was confined somehow. Confined within Marcus? Maybe that was what Zelden meant when he said he couldn't contain it. Maybe the Watcher was breaking out. And if that happened, he would head for the one place where he knew he could find me: school.

I searched my desk for Beth's business card. It was too early to call her, but I wanted to keep the card handy. I had a gnawing sense that I might need it soon.

Knowing that there was zero chance of my getting back to sleep, I decided to get ready for school. After a long, hot shower I dressed and went downstairs with the idea that I would surprise Mom with breakfast. She was already there, though, pouring her coffee at the counter.

"You're up early," she said with a yawn.

"Couldn't sleep." I poured myself a glass of grapefruit juice and grabbed a bagel from the fridge.

"I wanted to talk to you about something."

"Okay." I knew I should tell her about the phone call. She would take it seriously but not flip out over potential lawsuits, and then she and Beth could coordinate some kind of defense plan. I figured Zelden had taken Marcus away on a trip, possibly even out of the country, to keep his possessed assistant away from me. My dad might hate the guy, but I knew he was trying to help me somehow.

"I was thinking about spring break," she began. "How would you feel about the four of us taking a trip to visit Annalise in Charleston?"

"Dad, too?"

"Dad, too."

I was thrilled. Finally, my parents were making a step toward being together instead of living apart. Maybe that awful fight the week before hadn't broken them up. Maybe it had pushed them to realize that they needed to be together in order to work things out.

I decided not to tell Mom about Zelden's wake-up call. She would want to get involved, Dad would know and the fighting would begin all over again. I would not be the cause of that, I vowed, especially when they were so close to fixing everything. I needed to tell someone, but it wouldn't be Mom. Not yet, at least.

Avery arrived to pick me up for school. I tried to pay attention to her chatter as she drove us through our neighborhood and down Main Street, but really, I had no idea what she was talking about. At one point, she mentioned Plexiglas.

"Why do you need Plexiglas?" I asked.

"Not me." She looked over at me. "Jared bought the Plexiglas."

"Why is Jared buying Plexiglas?"

"Have you been listening to me at all?"

"No," I admitted. "I'm sorry. Lots on my mind right now."

Avery guided her Mini Cooper into the senior parking lot. We were early, and only a few people lingered outside. Avery cut the engine, but neither one of us got out of the car.

"What's going on?"

"Too much." I focused on the morning sky, which was streaked with shades of purple and pink. "I got a weird phone call this morning. Dr. Zelden thinks I may be in danger."

"Danger from what?"

"Marcus, I think. Or not Marcus, but the thing that was inside him."

"Sounds creepy."

"Welcome to my life. Creepy comes with the territory."

"What can I do to help? I'm here for you. Whatever you need, name it."

I felt lucky to have a best friend like Avery. "Thanks. What I need is a dose of normal, I think."

"And you came here?" Avery joked.

We walked into the building together. It still wasn't crowded yet, which I liked, but as I approached my locker, I saw that someone was standing there waiting for me.

"Bliss?"

I knew it was her, but at the same time, I felt like I had to ask because she wasn't dressed in her usual bright, solid colors. Instead, she was wearing faded jeans and a lumpy gray sweatshirt. And her hair, which I knew she typically took great care to ensure its shiny smooth perfection, was dull and frizzy. But what really made me question whether or not the real Bliss Reynolds was standing in front of me was her blank face, which was completely barren of any makeup.

"Are you okay?" Obviously, she was not, but it was the only thing I could think to ask.

"My grandfather died." She kept her eyes down.

"I'm so sorry."

"He'd been sick but we thought he was getting better. And then, last night…" Her voice trailed off.

"Is there anything I can do?" I meant it, even if I had no idea what I could do to help a grieving girl who could barely stand me.

"I'm going to be out of school for the week," Bliss said, her voice gaining strength. "I got here early today so I could get my books. I wanted to let you know that I already talked to Morley, and he said you could take over as anchor for the morning news."

"Oh. Okay." I absolutely did not want to take over for anything. I hated being in front of the camera. "Um, are you sure? I mean, can Morley find somebody else, maybe?"

The old Bliss resurfaced for a moment, her voice sharp. "Yeah, right. Don't pretend you haven't been waiting for the chance to step into my job, Charlotte. We both know that's a lie."

"Bliss, really, I don't want—"

She turned around and stormed away. I told myself that it wasn't really me she was angry with. She was upset over the death of her grandfather. Still, her harsh judgment of me stung. I would never be able to convince her that I did not place the same importance as she did on the school news.

"Was that Bliss?" Avery asked, coming up behind me.

"Yes. And she's mad at me again." I briefly filled her in. "Why does she care so much about ten minutes on the screen? Half the school doesn't even pay attention."

Avery shrugged. "It's all she has, I guess."

"That's depressing."

"What's depressing?" Harris joined us, smiling wide and reaching for my books.

"Bliss's grandfather died last night," I told him.

"Huh. Well, old people die. We still on for tomorrow night?"

I was annoyed by his casual response, but he didn't really know Bliss, so I could see how it wasn't a big deal to him. "Yeah, we're still on for tomorrow," I said. "Are you ready to tell me where we're going?"

"Nope."

Avery giggled. "Charlotte hates surprises." The first bell rang. "Have fun, you two!" she said as she hurried to first period. Harris walked me to class, nodding and smiling at people he knew in the hallway. As we passed by the library, he paused.

"Wonder what's going on?" He motioned toward the glass doors. Behind them, a throng of students had gathered. As we got closer, I could see that the library was a mess, books scattered everywhere.

"Someone trashed the library?" I asked out loud.

"Mind if we stop in?"

Harris opened the door for me. I was greeted with a chorus

of confused voices as people looked around trying to figure out what had happened.

"It was like this when I arrived this morning," the librarian, Mrs. Gladysz, wailed to the security guard.

I looked around. Hundreds of books surrounded us. They were all open, I realized. I knelt down to pick one up. Page fifty-five looked up at me.

"Didn't Bliss tell a story about this?" Harris whispered next to me.

"Yep." I looked at some of the other books on the floor. The ones I could see were all open to page fifty-five. I knew in my gut it was yet another elaborate prank, but I couldn't figure out who would be able to pull it off. Sneaking into a locked library at night, avoiding the security system and ravaging the shelves would take careful planning and more than a few hours.

And possibly more than one person.

The second bell rang, declaring that Harris and I were officially late for class. "Let's go," he said, steering me toward the doors. "Doc Larsen might let you off with a warning."

I knew my English teacher would shake her head and demand that I obtain a late pass from the main office. Five seconds late or five minutes—it didn't matter to her. Late was late. So when I saw Noah emerge from one of the bare stacks, I stopped. "Go ahead," I told Harris. "I'll get a pass."

He handed over my books and rushed out. I waved at Noah, who came over to me. "Can you believe this mess?" he asked. "Mrs. Gladysz is taking it personally. She thinks someone did this to hurt her."

"Why would anyone want to hurt her?" Mrs. Gladysz was a quiet, smiling woman who went out of her way to locate good books for the few students who actually approached her for something not required for class.

"This was Bliss's candle story, right?" Noah asked. "We should find her."

"She's not here," I said, my eyes still on Mrs. Gladysz. She was sitting in a chair, looking out at the library like it was a battlefield strewn with bodies. "Her grandfather passed away last night."

"I'm sorry to hear that," Noah said. "I thought I saw her, though, earlier this morning."

I turned my attention to Noah. He was wearing the red shirt again, the one that contrasted with his eyes, making them shine more green. "She came by to pick up her things. She'll be gone all week, though."

Noah nodded. "Okay, then." He looked over at the librarian. "I feel really bad for her. I wish I could do something."

"Maybe we can." I walked over to Mrs. Gladysz. "Can we help you pick up?" I asked.

"So many books," Mrs. Gladysz responded, her voice soft. "I don't care what the security guard said. This was not a harmless prank. This was malicious."

"We can come by during lunch," Noah offered.

Mrs. Gladysz looked up, surprised. "That would be nice. Thank you."

I didn't mind the fact that Noah had just volunteered us to spend our entire lunch period organizing books. In fact, I thought as I hurried to the main office to obtain a late slip, I was looking forward to it. It would give Noah and me a chance to talk more. AV class was not enough sometimes, and our conversations were constantly interrupted by people needing to watch footage or hand us discs.

I met up with Harris after first period and told him what I'd be doing. "Don't they have people to take care of that?" He frowned. "Like, you know, the custodian or someone?"

"It's a big job," I replied. "Extra hands will make it go faster."

Harris nodded, but he looked confused. "Did you get a chance to talk to your parents about Gwyn's house?"

"Not yet." I felt guilty, but I'd barely seen my parents in the past few days. Even though they were planning a family vacation to Charleston, they managed to avoid one another. They had choreographed a routine to make sure they were never in the same room at the same time, and I didn't want to risk asking one and infuriating the other, jeopardizing our spring break plans. "I'll ask as soon as I see them," I told Harris, but I knew that meant waiting a week.

I don't know why I looked forward to lunch. Spending forty-five minutes crouched on the library floor was not going to be enjoyable, but still, I found myself glancing at the clock often during third period. When the bell finally rang, I nearly raced toward the library. For the first time all day, I felt like I was moving toward something good. It didn't make sense, really. I wasn't headed toward anything special.

Just Noah.

# sixteen

Noah was already in the library when I got there, kneeling on the floor and shutting each book before he checked the spine and returned it to the correct shelf. He smiled when he saw me. "Ready for five kinds of fun?"

I looked around at the colossal disaster I had volunteered to tackle. "Only five kinds? Come on, this is at least nine."

Noah nodded toward some scattered dictionaries. "I saved those for you. I'll finish here and we can meet in the middle."

I got right to work. There were a ton of dictionaries, but they all went in the same spot, so I didn't have to sort through them as carefully as Noah did with his random stack of novels. It was quiet in the library. Mrs. Gladysz walked around with a clipboard, making notes about which shelves were missing books and double-checking to make sure that the books still on the floor hadn't been damaged.

"How's it going over there?" Noah asked.

I had finished shelving a few dozen heavy dictionaries. "My arms are getting a good workout," I replied. "You?"

"I think I'm going blind from reading the little numbers on the spines of these things."

Mrs. Gladysz came over to us. She held her clipboard against her chest and beamed. "You've already made such wonderful progress! Thank you so much!"

"No problem, Mrs. G," Noah said. "We'll work on nonfiction next."

"Very good. I'm going to lunch, but I'll be back before the end of the period."

"Where's nonfiction?" I asked after Mrs. Gladysz left. Noah led the way to a corner of the library. There were fewer books strewn across the floor, so I knew we could clean it up within a few minutes.

"Something's been bothering me," Noah said as he closed books.

"Really? But everything has been so normal around here," I joked.

Noah shook his head. He placed a book back on the shelf, then sat down on the floor. "The cell phone incident," he began. "It's the one story that wasn't told at the party, and it's the one thing that caused the most disruption here. Any theories?"

"None," I admitted. "And it's weird, because that was the same day Zelden called me for the first time."

"The demon guy called you?" Noah frowned. "What did he want?"

I shut an open book. "I don't know, exactly. My dad intercepted the call."

"You said it was the first time he called. So he's called you again?"

"This morning, actually."

I stopped shelving and told Noah everything. It felt good to confide in him, to share the details as clearly as I could recall them. I kept my voice low in case anyone else was in the library, but sitting on the floor with Noah, it felt like we were the only two people in the school. After I described Zelden's calls, I explained that I hadn't yet told my parents anything because I didn't want to endanger their possible reunion.

He was looking down at the floor. "So you're saying that basically, there's an evil force heading in this direction and that its one and only goal is to punish you?"

"Um, yeah. I guess that sums it up."

"And your parents are clueless and no one is actively doing anything to protect you right now? What about Harris? You told him, right?"

I fidgeted with my amethyst necklace. "It's too complicated. He wouldn't understand."

"You're killing me, Charlotte." Noah ran a hand through his hair. "You're in serious danger and you're acting like it's not a big deal. I saw your arm in that sling. I know what Marcus was able to do in under a minute. If he gets his hands on you again…"

"I know, but Zelden said he's far away. And spring break is in two days. I'll tell my parents while we're in Charleston, okay?"

"But Marcus could show up here in the next two days."

"I'll be careful."

"Careful how?" Noah was obviously agitated. He kept messing with his hair. "You need protection. I'll keep my eyes open for strangers around school, but there's only so much I can do to keep you safe."

I don't know why it thrilled me to hear him say that he wanted to keep me safe. We were friends—of course he wanted me to be safe. But the way he said it, like my security mattered to him, well, it made me want to hug him. Maybe more than hug. I wanted to feel his arms around me.

"It's just two days. I'll be fine."

"Yeah?" Noah's gaze went to my neck. "You only play with that necklace when you're worried about something."

I immediately let go of the amethyst. "That's not true!"

"Yes, it is. I've seen you. Every time you get upset, your hand goes right to it."

"Yeah, well, every time you're upset you run your hands through your hair."

We stared at each other for a moment. Then Noah laughed. "I know, I know. Nervous habit." I relaxed, but then Noah reached for my hand. "I'm worried about you Charlotte, I really am. Promise you'll tell me if you see or feel anything weird."

"I promise." I tried to ignore how warm his hand felt on mine. "But promise me you won't tell my parents or Shane."

"Only if you promise you *will* tell them over break."

"Deal." I didn't want him to let go of my hand, but we still had work to do. By the time the lunch bell rang, we had cleared about half the floor of books and earned eternal appreciation from Mrs. Gladysz, who happily wrote us late-passes.

Noah walked me to class. "This isn't necessary," I protested.

"Over the next two days you're going to say that a lot," he replied. "But for me, it is necessary. So don't bother fighting with me. You'll lose."

"Fine." I tried to sound annoyed, but it was hard to hide how pleased I was.

The next two days flew by more quickly than I thought possible. It wasn't just the onslaught of pre-break tests that the teachers loved to throw at us; it was also the fact that I was now the temporary anchor of the school news, a job I absolutely hated. I complained until Morley agreed to let one of the freshman guys co-anchor with me, but the boy was so nervous he could do little more than offer a nervous smile the moment the lights came on. I was determined not to overshadow Bliss, so I wore jeans and neutral shirts and did my best to look as unpolished as possible. Despite my efforts to be entirely forgettable, though, people kept complimenting me on my "natural" way in front of the camera. Harris, in particular, was thrilled.

"People love you!" he said as we walked to class together. And although I felt safe with his strong arm securely planted on my shoulder, I felt even better knowing that Noah was nearby. Every time I turned around, Noah was there, taking the long way to class to make sure he saw me.

Another person who always seemed to be around was Gwyn. I didn't ask Harris about her directly, but I thought that they had probably gotten over their fight the night of the basketball game and that he had told her that I would try to get my parents to reinvestigate her home. She didn't talk to me, but I noticed the dark circles under her eyes when we were in class and the way she lingered at her locker, staring into it as if she couldn't remember what books she needed.

Friday finally arrived. I was relieved that nothing strange had happened since the library incident, happy that I would no longer be forced to read the school news, and excited that spring break was only hours away.

"How's our celebrity news anchor?" Avery asked me at lunch. The cafeteria was less congested than usual. A lot of people had decided to begin their break early.

I groaned. "Not funny. I can't wait to get back to editing and leave the interviews to Bliss."

"Come on, you're great! That piece you did on the vegetarian nuggets was a hit."

I poked at my soggy tuna fish sandwich. "Maybe I should have gotten those for lunch today instead of this."

"Just think, though—this time tomorrow you'll be dining on real seafood in Charleston."

I smiled. "Shrimp and grits. My favorite." I pushed the sandwich aside. "I wish you weren't going to be stuck here."

Avery nibbled at a carrot stick. "It won't be so bad. My mom's taking a few days off so we can go shopping." She looked around at the small crowd of students eating their lunch. "Have you seen Jared today?"

"No." I hadn't seen Harris, either. The only person I kept running into was Noah, who always seemed both panicked and relieved to find me in one piece.

"I thought he'd be finished with the memorial by now," Avery said.

"The one-year anniversary isn't until the Monday after break, though, right?"

"Yes. I guess I thought he'd be done early." She sighed. "Not that I'm looking forward to it."

I was surprised. "You're not?"

"I mean, I want to see what Jared's been working on, but it just reminds me that this horrible date is approaching." She stared at her carrot sticks. "One full year since Adam died. It doesn't seem possible."

"I'm sorry. I wish I'd known him."

Avery smiled. "He would have liked you." She wrapped up the rest of her uneaten lunch. "Enough sad stuff. I'm coming over tonight to help you pack. And I'm expecting a cool souvenir when you return."

"Done. One glitter-encrusted plastic crab coming your way."

The rest of my classes were only half-full and the teachers showed movies while they sat at their desks. I saw Harris before the end of the day, and he asked me to meet him by the back doors when school was over. "I have something for you," he said with a wink. When the final bell rang, I stuffed everything in my locker, grabbed my jacket, and was standing by the doors before most people had a chance to leave their classrooms.

Soon the hallways were empty, but I was still waiting. I heard running footsteps approach me and looked toward them, expecting Harris, but it was Noah.

"I think he's here," he gasped.

"Who's here?"

"Marcus." He paused to catch his breath. "There's a strange guy walking around, looking into classrooms."

I felt a chill pass through me and immediately touched my necklace. "Are you sure it's him?"

"I never met the guy, so no, I'm not sure. But I've never seen him before and he has dark hair. I'm getting you away from here. Let's go." He put his hand on the small of my back and gently pushed me toward the doors.

"Sorry I'm late." Harris jogged up to us. When he saw Noah touching me, he frowned. "Everything okay?"

I froze. What was I supposed to say to him?

Noah let his hand drop. "Hey, Harris. I want to get Charlotte out of here. I thought I saw one of her family's creepy fans wandering around the school. They can be a little intense, you know?"

Harris turned to me. "Is someone bothering you?"

"Um, well, there's this guy—" I began.

"Where is he?" he asked, his voice hard.

"I saw him by the science labs a couple minutes ago," Noah said. "Tall guy, dark hair."

"That him?"

Noah and I spun around. A man was walking slowly down

the hallway, peering into the open classrooms. My first thought was that it wasn't Marcus, but it had been a while since I'd seen him. I couldn't make out his face, but the height was about right. I tensed.

"That's him," Noah whispered.

"Hey!" Harris yelled. The man stopped and looked at us, then began walking faster in our direction.

Noah stepped in front of me. "Are you crazy?"

I squeezed my eyes shut and stayed behind Noah, one hand on his back and the other clutching my necklace. It wasn't warm or tingling or doing anything that Beth had said it might do. It was just a rock, as powerless as I was.

"Hey, coach."

I opened my eyes. Harris was shaking hands with the mysterious guy, and now that I saw him up close, I realized he wasn't Marcus; in fact, the only resemblance was the height and hair color.

Harris introduced us. "This is the new JV coach," he explained. "You lost?"

The coach laughed. "I think so. I'm supposed to talk to a teacher in room one thirteen."

"That way." Harris pointed. "All the way down the hall, then turn right."

After the coach had left, Harris put his arm around my shoulders. "You didn't need to scare Charlotte like that," he said to Noah.

"I'm sorry," Noah stammered. "I'd never seen him before and—"

"Well, maybe you would have recognized him if you spent more time sitting in the bleachers instead of crawling around under them."

Noah clenched his fists and Harris stood a little taller, and I stepped in between them before things escalated. "Noah was just looking out for me," I said calmly. "No harm done." The guys were staring hard at each other. I tried to appeal to Harris. "Please. We're about to leave on break. I won't see you for over a week."

Harris broke his stare and smiled at me. "That's right. And I have something for you." He pulled a small black box from his jacket. Noah was still standing there, watching us. I opened the box and pulled out the necklace inside. At the end of a thin gold chain was a single pearl.

"So you have something else to wear besides that big rock," Harris explained, nodding toward my neck.

I smiled. "It's lovely. Thank you."

"Here, let me put it on you." Harris moved behind me, nudging Noah out of the way, and gingerly clasped the jewelry. Then he kissed the back of my neck softly, making me shiver a little. "Think about me over the break, okay?"

Noah cleared his throat. "I should go."

Harris grinned. "No, stay. I have to get home, and Charlotte might need someone around to protect her from the girls' volleyball coach." He winked, then gave me a kiss on the cheek before striding through the doors.

"I'm so sorry," I said to Noah. "He's not usually like that."

"Right." Noah's face was red, and I wasn't sure if it was from embarrassment or rage.

I didn't know what else I could say. "Do you have a ride home?" I asked.

"I missed my bus." He wasn't even looking at me. I felt so guilty. I had put him in an uncomfortable moment and I didn't know how to make it right.

"Noah—"

"Is that Jared?" Noah was looking past me. I turned around and, sure enough, there was Jared near some lockers at the end of the hallway. He waved and came toward us. His limp, which had been so pronounced a few months earlier, seemed less noticeable now.

"I was looking for you," he said to me. He looked happy and excited, a rare combination for him. "It's done."

"You finished the memorial? That's great!"

"You busy right now? I want you to see it." He smiled at Noah. "You, too, if you want."

"Yeah, if you can give me a ride home afterwards."

Jared nodded. "Sure. Might be a tight squeeze, though."

We walked out to the parking lot. "I didn't know you had a car," I said.

"I've been borrowing my dad's truck for a while," Jared explained. "I needed it to haul supplies."

We came to a red pickup. "You needed a truck? How big is the memorial?"

He smiled. "Big."

I sat between Jared and Noah. It was warm inside the truck's cab, and I was acutely aware of Noah's scent, which was a combination of the cinnamon gum he liked to chew and some kind of musky aftershave.

As Jared drove I began growing excited that I would finally see what he had been working on for so long. We pulled into the driveway of a green ranch house a few miles from my own neighborhood. Jared stopped in front of the garage and turned off the ignition. "It's set up in the garage," he said. We got out of the truck and stood in front of the closed door. Jared held the remote opener in his hand.

"Ready?" he asked.

Noah and I nodded. Jared hit the button, and the garage door began to open with a rusty squeal. When it was all the way up, we were facing the memorial. I sucked in my breath.

"Wow," Noah breathed.

We entered the garage slowly. I tried to take in everything I was seeing, but it was so massive, so detailed, I knew I could stand there for hours and not read everything that covered it.

"What do you guys think?" Jared asked. There was a note of worry in his voice.

I felt a tear sting the corner of my eye. "Oh, Jared." I walked around the memorial, knowing there was even more to see. Finally, I looked at him.

"Well?" he asked. "Do you think Avery will like it?"

I knew what he wanted my answer to be, but only one thing came to my mind and out of my mouth. "I think it will break her heart."

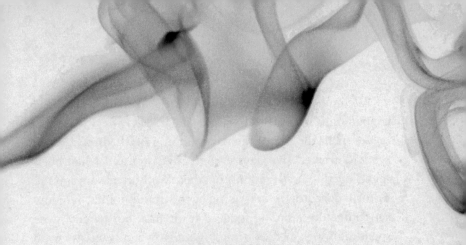

# seventeen

"It was amazing," I told Annalise.

"Sounds amazing."

We were lying on our beach towels, soaking up the bright Charleston sunshine. I closed my eyes and listened to the overzealous gulls and gently lapping waves. It was the most relaxed I'd felt in months.

"It's going to be great when everyone comes back next week and sees Jared's memorial on the front lawn," I continued. "I hope the school appreciates it. I was blown away, and I didn't even know Adam."

I wasn't describing the memorial well enough to do it justice. Jared had taken mammoth sheets of Plexiglas to create three walls, each about seven feet high. The center wall featured a poster of Adam wearing his football uniform. Surrounding the poster were notes and cards people had left in front of Adam's locker after he died and other mementos Jared had secretly collected. The Plexiglas held them suspended, and we could walk around to read the backs of notes. There was a museum-like quality to it, a sense that the walls held priceless artifacts. And in a way, they did.

"Well, make sure to send me pictures," Annalise said as she flipped onto her back. "I want to see it."

We spent the rest of the day lounging on the beach. Since we had arrived five days earlier, my sister and I had been spending all our afternoons together. We walked through the historic downtown, marveling at the grand homes, window shopping and sampling fudge. Meanwhile, our parents were spending much-needed time together. It had been awkward initially. Our first dinner together was strained, with Mom and Dad acting like strangers who weren't sure what to say to one another. The second day was better, with a little more conversation. I stayed at Annalise's apartment while our parents shared a hotel room. We met them for breakfast and dinner each day, but for the most part, we wanted them to be alone.

Harris called me on the third day of our trip. I was alone in Annalise's tiny apartment while she was out with Mills, so it was the perfect opportunity to ask him to be nicer to Noah.

"The thing is, his mom is dating my, um, uncle," I said, knowing it would be too difficult to explain my exact relationship with Shane.

"Okay. But he's around you a lot. Every time I see you, he's standing a few feet away. It's like he's obsessed."

"Trust me, he's not." I touched the tiny pearl that Harris had given me. I was wearing it alongside my amethyst. Even though I didn't believe the amethyst could do anything to protect me, I had gotten used to the weight of it, and it made Mom happy. Sometimes the pearl clinked against the large purple rock, but most of the time it rested behind it, hidden.

"I'll be nicer, I promise," he said. There was a pause. "I really miss you. Have you had a chance to talk to your parents about Gwyn's house?"

"I told them about it last night." It wasn't a conversation I wanted to have with them, but I knew Harris was counting on me, so I had brought it up over dessert. They were in a particularly good mood as they tasted each other's slices of cake, and I noticed they were sitting closer to one another at the table.

"There's this girl at school," I began. "And she's having some problems with her house. She thinks it's haunted."

Mom licked chocolate icing from her fork. "Why does she think that?"

"After her family began renovations, furniture moved. She feels something there."

"Feelings are often misleading," Dad said. "Might be an electrical problem."

Mom poked her fork into Dad's cake, and he pretended to swat at her hand. "Charlotte, if your friend is having trouble, we'd be happy to help."

Gwyn wasn't my friend, exactly. She was a girl I knew, a girl who was connected to Harris. I wasn't doing this for her. I was doing this for my future prom date.

"Thanks," I said to my parents. "It would mean a lot to me."

That was the truth. It meant more to Harris, and I didn't want to disappoint him. I told my parents I would give them the details after we returned home.

"So make sure I have her full name and address," I told Harris when he called. "And if my parents gave her a case file, they'll need that number."

"Thank you so much, Charlotte." Harris sounded happy and relieved. "You're the best. I'm going to call Gwyn right now."

I was pleased with myself for keeping a promise to Harris, but I hadn't yet fulfilled my promise to Noah. My parents still didn't know anything about Zelden's phone calls. Although his warnings chilled me to the bone, I felt safe in Charleston, away from my house and surrounded by my family. Marcus couldn't find me here, I was sure of it. And I wanted to wait as long as possible before breaking the news and making everyone worried.

"It's going really well, don't you think?" I asked Annalise. We were sharing a picnic lunch at the base of the same ancient tree where we'd seen the lights months earlier. I had hoped to feel something when we sat down, but I didn't. It was just a tree.

"Yeah." Annalise unscrewed the top from a bottle of green tea. "I think they've turned a corner, I really do."

"It happened so fast," I continued, picking at the wrapper of a granola bar I'd brought with me. "Everything was fine and then suddenly it wasn't."

"Do you really believe it happened like that?"

"You don't?"

She set down her tea in the grass. "Charlotte, I think they've been very careful for years not to reveal their problems to us. Whatever happened here last fall only brought out something that was already there."

"Like the dormant energy Dad is always talking about?"

Annalise smiled. "That's a good way of looking at it."

"So now that the dormant energy has been stirred up, they can deal with it," I said, more to myself than my sister. She heard me, though, and nodded.

"Now we can all deal with it."

The next few days of our trip felt like a real family vacation. Every day seemed to bring my parents closer together. They held hands during a late-night walk near the beach. They laughed as we sampled confections at one of the tiny sweet shops downtown. I even witnessed Dad whispering something in Mom's ear that made her giggle and turn away, blushing.

Annalise and I shared our own knowing looks, confident that the issues between our parents had been resolved. "If I'd known that all they needed was a vacation, I would have suggested this a lot earlier," Annalise said. It was our last night in Charleston, and we were getting ready to meet our parents for dinner. I was tense because I planned on telling them about Zelden's calls, but I tried not to think about it too much.

"I can't do anything with my hair!" Annalise announced.

"It looks great." I didn't need to look—her hair always looked glossy and full.

"I need ten more minutes." Annalise disappeared into the bathroom while I stayed in the living room and cleaned out my purse. It was full of wrinkled receipts and gum wrappers. I dumped everything out and sorted the garbage from the things I might actually need later. I was debating whether or not to keep a half-empty and slightly melted tube of passion-fruit lip gloss when my phone buzzed.

"Charlotte? It's Dr. Zelden."

I felt panic at the sound of his voice and braced myself for the impossible news that Marcus had somehow made his way to Charleston. I touched my amethyst.

"Is everything okay?" I managed to ask.

"Yes, dear. Everything is fine." He coughed. "I am calling to let you know that the situation with Marcus has been, um, resolved."

The way he stressed the last word made me immediately think that something bad had happened. "Is he dead?" I blurted out.

Another cough. "No, Marcus is not dead."

"Good." As much as Marcus had terrified me, I knew he was innocent. There was something inside him, separate from him. But it wasn't him. I wondered how Dr. Zelden had managed to get rid of the Watcher.

"I must go now," Zelden said. "But I wonder if you would do me a favor?"

"Favor?" I had no idea what I could do for Zelden. I didn't even know where he was, although his voice did not sound as distant and filled with static as it had in previous calls.

"I need you to pass along a message to your mother."

"Sure, Dr. Zelden." I couldn't imagine what he would have to say to my mother. They hadn't spoken to one another since Christmas.

"It's very important. Please tell her that I am terribly sorry, but the amethyst has broken."

"Okay."

"You will tell her, won't you?"

"Of course."

He coughed again. It was a dry, hacking sound. "Thank you, dear. And Charlotte?"

"Yes?"

"It was nice to have met you."

"You, too, Dr. Zelden."

But he had already hung up.

# eighteen

The Monday after break was clear and green and warm, a sublime mixture of spring slipping into early summer. I was up extra early, and as I came downstairs after my shower, everything felt right in my world. Mom and Dad were in the kitchen sipping their coffee and reading an open newspaper on the table.

"Good morning!" Dad said. He was downright cheerful, and I found myself smiling, despite the fact that it was barely seven in the morning.

"Noah's coming home with you after school," Mom informed me. "Trisha's going to be working here all day."

My good mood faded slightly. "But Harris is giving me a ride home today."

I did not want to create another awkward encounter between Harris and Noah. I wondered if I could get Avery to give us a ride home instead. I heard two honks of a car horn outside and went to the window.

"Avery's here," I announced. I glanced at the clock. "She's a half hour early." I gathered up my things, swiped a banana off the counter and waved good-bye to my parents.

"Someone's eager to get to school today," I joked as I slid into the passenger seat of Avery's green Mini Cooper.

"Well, yeah, have you forgotten?" She looked into the rearview mirror as she guided her car down my driveway.

"Jared's memorial!" It had slipped my mind. Jared had planned to have it up and ready on the school's front lawn when the student body returned from break.

"I can't believe you've seen it and I haven't," Avery continued.

"Are you going to be okay?" I asked gently. Jared had chosen this day to reveal his work because it marked the one-year anniversary of Adam's death.

Avery came to a stop sign. "I've been dreading this day," she said. "But it's here and I have to deal with it. This is the day he died, but I've decided not to let it overshadow all the days he lived."

I touched her arm. "You're strong, you know that?"

Avery drove on. "Yeah, well, we'll see how strong I am after I get a look at the memorial."

There were no other cars in the senior parking lot, but I spotted Jared's red truck on the street, parked near the school's front entrance. Avery and I walked across the parking lot and toward the front lawn. I saw Jared, hands shoved in his pockets as he stood back and gazed up at his work, which was partially blocked by a tree. Avery slowed her pace as we got closer, as if afraid to finally face Jared's tribute and what it represented. But a few more steps, and we were there, standing in front of the three clear walls and the memorabilia they held.

We stood there, silent. Avery's face was hard to read. She leaned in closer, taking in each wall with its notes and pictures. Her fingers rested on the middle wall, where Adam's football jersey was preserved in Plexiglas, directly beneath the full-color poster of Adam himself.

"How did you do this?" she asked.

Jared moved next to Avery so they were standing side by side. I hung back, watching. "Some of it I collected after he died." He pointed to a group of cards and dried flowers. "They were left at his grave. I got the jersey from his parents."

"You talked to them? After they moved, I didn't know how to get in touch."

"I found them. At first, they didn't want to see me. But after a while…"

I understood then what Jared had meant when he'd said he wasn't working alone on his project. I couldn't imagine the courage it took to contact two grieving people who blamed you for their son's death. But Jared had done it.

After a while, cars started pulling into the parking lot and the lawn swelled with curious students. They were quiet as they took in the walls, respectful. They walked around it, reading the cards and pointing to pictures. Jared, Avery and I left the crowd and went inside the school, which was nearly empty. Everyone else was outside, admiring the memorial.

"So you like it?" Jared asked Avery nervously.

"I love it." Avery pulled Jared into a hug. The first bell rang, but I doubt either of them heard it. Then people began filling the hallway, and they both stepped back, their eyes shiny. They didn't say anything else. They didn't have to.

Harris was waiting for me after first-period English. "I missed you," he said, wrapping his arms around me.

"Missed you, too." I touched my necklace, the round pearl so light that I barely felt it at my neck. After Zelden's call I had placed the amethyst in my purse, right next to Beth's business card for Potion.

Harris reached into his pocket and retrieved a folded piece of paper. "Here's Gwyn's info." I glanced at it. A case number was typed at the top, with Gwyn's address, 530 Woodlyn, beneath it. We began walking toward my next class. "Thanks so much for convincing your parents to check out her house."

I hadn't really convinced them of anything. They didn't know yet that I was asking them to look into a house they had already seen and declared fine. I put the paper in my purse. "I'll give this to them when I get home. Are you still planning on giving me a ride?"

"I have a better idea," he said. He stopped in front of my classroom. "How about we go out after school? I was thinking pizza at Giuseppe's."

"Actually, I need a favor. Noah's coming over to my house after school."

Harris frowned. "Why is Noah going to your house?"

"His mom works for my mom. They'll be there, too." I don't know why I felt I needed to point out that there would be parents present, but it seemed necessary.

"Okay," Harris said after a pause. "How about this? Instead of going out after school, I pick you up for dinner around five? We can catch up, spend some time together. Think Avery can give you a ride home?"

"I can find a ride." If I couldn't, Noah and I could always take the bus. I didn't like to see Harris so obviously upset by the idea of Noah spending time at my house, and it bothered me that Harris didn't even want to be in the same car with Noah, but I knew it was for the best. Tension had been averted, at least for now.

The memorial was big news throughout the day, even eclipsing conversations about spring break parties and the search for supernatural activity in the school. Nothing had happened over break, though. Not one locker opened or chair moved or strange security footage shot. I was relieved, but it also made me wonder about the timing. Everything had stopped at the same time Zelden had told me that the Watcher was gone.

Had the incidents at school really been paranormal? Or was there still a culprit to be caught?

I saw Bliss before fourth period, dressed head to toe in daisy-yellow, a freshman boy in tow as she marched outside to film the memorial. I was glad to see her back at school. People had been asking me if I would take over the school news, a question I always answered with an emphatic no. I was more than happy to hand over all anchoring duties to Bliss.

Avery was in a good mood at lunch. She was a little quieter than usual, but she told me that Bliss had interviewed her for a piece about the walls. "I told her I thought it was a wonderful reminder that Adam lived a great life," she said. "And I invited people to add to it, if they wanted. I'm going to bring in some pictures from home."

I was able to watch the interview in AV class. Noah wasn't there yet, so I loaded the disc and began reviewing the footage and planning how we could edit it to fit two minutes. I heard the tapping of heels on linoleum and looked up to see Bliss enter the room. I got up so I could talk to her.

"I'm really glad you're back," I said.

"Are you?" Bliss glared at me. "I hear that you did a fabulous job taking over for me. I've been hearing it all day. Well done."

It was a bitter compliment, and I wasn't sure how to respond. I was angry, but I knew she was still grieving over the death of her grandfather and I didn't want to say anything sharp.

"Well, I'm glad it's over and I'm happy you're back in front of the camera," I said. "Avery told me you did a great interview. I'm going to begin editing it now."

Bliss softened a little. "Jared did an amazing job. I just want the story to capture that."

"I'll do my best," I promised.

Noah arrived. It was the first time I'd seen him since spring break. While we worked on editing, he asked me if I'd told my parents about Zelden's warning.

"Didn't have to," I said gleefully. "Zelden called again and said everything was fine."

"Just like that?"

"Just like that." He'd also asked me to pass along a message to Mom, but I had decided to wait on passing it on so we could enjoy dinner together as a family.

"How was your break?" I asked Noah.

He sighed and said that it basically had involved a lot of uncomfortable evenings with his mom and Shane. "He's trying too hard," Noah complained. "He kept bringing over DVDs he thought I'd like. He wanted us to bond."

"Is that really so bad?"

"I don't want to bond with him. I don't need a dad."

"I don't think he's trying to be your dad," I said carefully. "He just wants you guys to get along, you know?"

"We can get along from a distance." Noah's voice was final, so I dropped the subject.

"You're coming home with me today," I informed him. "Avery's giving us a ride."

"Yeah, my mom told me this morning." He turned his attention back to the computer. "This is a great story. I'm impressed."

"With the memorial or Bliss's interview?"

"Both." He glanced at the wall clock. "Let's get this done."

We finished the story minutes before the bell rang. I was pleased with our work. We'd added music to the background, and overlaid student interviews with wide shots of the three walls. I described it to Avery as she drove us to my house.

When she dropped off Noah and me, she said she was heading back to the school.

"I want to add more pictures and maybe some flowers," she said. "We have permission to keep it up all week, and I'm hoping it grows."

After Avery left, I turned to Noah. "We may have more editing in our future because of this."

We went inside. "So far, this is the best thing we've worked on," he said. "I wouldn't mind a few more features like this one."

My mom and Trisha were in the living room. Trisha was reading aloud email messages while Mom sorted through papers. "When was the last one dated?" Mom asked.

Trisha clicked on a message. "Last week, just before you left for vacation."

"And it came from New Zealand?"

I overheard this last part as I was setting down my purse. "Cool! Are we taking a trip to New Zealand?"

Mom looked up. "I didn't hear you come in." She smiled. "Hi, Noah. And no, Charlotte, we are not going to New Zealand. I'm corresponding with someone there, that's all."

I pretended to pout. "But we could spend our next vacation in New Zealand!"

Mom chuckled. "We were gone for six days and I'm now trying to catch up on over four hundred emails," she said. "Next time, our vacation will be one weekend only."

Trisha talked with Noah as I grabbed a snack from the kitchen. When I returned, Mom was holding a large white box while Trisha grinned.

"This came for you today," Mom said. Obviously, she already knew what was in the wide, flat box. I was suspicious as she and Trisha ushered me into the dining room. Noah headed off to the kitchen. I sat on the sofa and opened the box, then peeled back crinkly layers of white tissue paper until I revealed the orange dress I had admired in Potion.

"Wow." It was even more gorgeous than I remembered. The embroidered bodice sparkled with tiny clear stones and the smooth fabric of the layered skirt felt luxurious in my hands. I looked at Mom. "How did you know?"

She beamed. "Beth thought you might like it for prom. She sent it over while we were gone."

"Try it on," Trisha urged.

Prom was still a month away, but holding the dress in my hands made it feel closer. I had a date and now a dress. I wasn't sure how I would be able to wait four weeks for the big event.

I went upstairs and slipped into the gown. It fit almost perfectly. The skirt was a little too long, but other than that, it felt like I was being hugged in all the right places. As I descended the stairs, I felt regal.

"You look fantastic!" Trisha exclaimed.

Mom was smiling, too. "It's beautiful."

Trisha grabbed her camera and ordered Mom to stand next to me for a picture. "My hair isn't right!" I protested, but Trisha wouldn't hear it. Mom put her arm around my waist, we both said cheese, and Trisha snapped a few shots. It felt silly, but I kind of loved the attention. They fussed over the skirt, which they agreed needed hemming. While they were examining the hemline, Noah walked in munching on an apple. He stopped chewing when he saw me.

"Whoa."

"It's my prom dress," I said. "I was just trying it on."

"Isn't she lovely, Noah?" Trisha prodded.

He simply nodded and returned to the kitchen. The phone rang and Mom answered it while Trisha advised me on how

I should wear my hair. "You could let it grow out a little, and then put it up," she suggested.

"Do you think there's time for it to grow long enough?" My hair barely hung past my earlobes.

"We could get extensions, maybe."

Mom rushed into the room, the phone pressed against her ear. "Uh-huh. Have you called Beth already?" She put one hand over the receiver. "It's Lisa. Looks like we're out of time."

Trisha raced to the living room, where she grabbed a black duffel bag. "I'm ready," she announced.

Noah emerged from the kitchen. "What's going on?"

"Just a little paranormal emergency, sweetie," Trisha said. "We'll be back later." She kissed his forehead. "Do your homework."

Mom hung up and snatched her purse and keys from the foyer table. "Have you called Shane?"

Trisha punched numbers on her phone. "Doing it now." She pressed the phone against her ear. "Hi, hon. You ready? It's go time." She walked toward the door as she spoke. "Do you have the address? It's 530 Woodlyn."

I watched as Mom and Trisha hurried toward the foyer. "What do I tell Dad?"

Mom stopped. "I'll call him later."

I had no idea where they were going, but I remembered the name Lisa from when Mom and I had gone to Potion. Lisa was the woman buying up everything in the shop. She must have been dealing with something scary—and active enough to draw Mom in.

"See you in a few hours!" Mom hollered as she and Trisha raced out the front door. It slammed shut, and a moment later we heard her car start up.

I turned to Noah. "So."

"So this is a typical afternoon in the Silver house."

I laughed. "Kind of. I'm starving. You want something else to eat?"

We raided the fridge and came up with enough ingredients to make turkey sandwiches. I sliced tomatoes while Noah got the bread and cheese.

"You planning on taking off that dress?" he asked. His eyes widened as soon as he said it. "I didn't mean, uh," he stammered. "I mean, are you going to change into something else?"

"In a little while." I was having too much fun walking around in my new gown, but I would definitely need to change before Harris arrived. I decided to make a smaller sandwich so I wouldn't be too full when Harris and I went out to dinner.

"I was thinking about the cell numbers," Noah said. "The four digits that showed up on everyone's phones at school?"

"Mmm," I said, my mouth full.

"What if it's a date? You know, zero four one three could be April thirteenth."

"That's tomorrow." I brushed some crumbs from my dress. I needed to be more careful. "Do you think that something big has been planned for tomorrow?"

Noah shrugged. "Maybe. Just a thought."

"Well," I said as I picked at my sandwich, "Harris and I are going out tonight. I'll ask him to drive by the school, see if anything is going on."

"Right." Noah was staring at his plate. "So I guess he's your prom date?"

"Yes." I sat a little straighter in my fabulous new dress. "He asked me before spring break."

"Well, he's a lucky guy." Noah's eyes met mine. "I mean it. You look…"

I was waiting for something bland, like *beautiful* or *pretty*. But Noah surprised me.

"You look radiant."

Radiant. No one had ever called me that before. "Thank you," I said softly. It was a sincere compliment, I could tell. "I should change before I get mayo all over it."

As I got up, my cell phone rang in the next room. I dug through my purse and picked up on the last ring.

"Charlotte?" It was Harris.

"Hey," I said. "I was just talking about you. When will you be here?"

"That's the thing." I could hear a strange commotion in the background and wondered if Harris was at some kind of protest march. There were a lot of voices chanting.

"Can we go out tomorrow? Something's come up. I'm really sorry."

"Oh." I had been looking forward to our dinner date. I thought he had been, as well. "I guess we could do it tomorrow."

"Thanks. You're the best. I have to go now."

"Wait," I said. "Where are you? Is everything okay?"

The voices in the background were getting louder. "Yeah. I'm okay. I'll see you tomorrow."

Before Harris hung up, I heard a voice rise above the rest, a voice chanting something unfamiliar. It was a voice I'd known all my life.

It was my mother's.

# nineteen

"Explain to me again why we're stealing my mom's car?" Noah asked.

I was still wearing my prom dress. I'd thrown on some old running shoes, grabbed Noah by the arm and basically ordered him to take his mom's car. Now I was fumbling with my purse, searching for the slip of paper Harris had given me earlier at school. My hand brushed against the amethyst necklace and I automatically squeezed it. I answered Noah's question.

"We're catching a ghost."

The hallways of Lincoln High had been haunted by the same spirit for months. As Noah drove his mom's car across town, I ran through a mental list of some of the "haunted" happenings: the ghost dog that had appeared within hours of Harris telling his story, the sound of footsteps, the clocks moving, the scent of peaches in the junior hallway, the power outages, the library books scattered across the floor. One thing connected them all, and now I had a name for my ghost.

Her name was Gwyn.

"Everything started with the party at Gwyn's house," I said to Noah. "She's behind everything."

"Why?"

I was still piecing it all together, but I explained what I had figured out so far. My parents had been to Gwyn's house before Christmas and decided it wasn't active enough to investigate. Gwyn's mom, Lisa, had stayed in touch with my mom and spent a lot of time and money at Potion. As things got worse, Gwyn became desperate. She needed help, and had decided that if I believed something real was happening at school, I'd convince my parents to go back to Gwyn's house, where the stories had all originated.

"Okay, let's say that's true." Noah turned off the main road. I had found the slip of paper with Gwyn's address written on it and directed Noah that way. "How did she manage to pull off everything?"

"She's been working in the main office all year." I told him how one day, the secretaries had been searching for the master keys. Gwyn had taken them, made copies and then placed them in the trash. "So she had total access to the school," I explained. "She probably knew all the codes and could come and go whenever she wanted."

"Still," Noah said. "How did she do it all by herself? Moving every chair, opening the lockers? That's a lot of work."

"You think she had help?"

"It's more than possible."

"But who?"

We had entered Gwyn's neighborhood, but instead of driving directly to the house, Noah pulled over on a side street and put the car in park.

"I need to tell you something," he said. "Maybe I should have earlier, but I wasn't sure if it meant anything."

His voice was serious, yet gentle, and I knew that whatever he was going to say, I wouldn't like it.

"I saw Harris and Gwyn together at homecoming."

"What do you mean, you saw them together?"

"In the parking lot. They were, uh, close."

Avery had told me that Harris had been busted making out with someone, but he had later told me it was just a rumor. "Well, it was before he knew me, so why does it matter?"

"Maybe it doesn't, "Noah said. "Maybe it was a one-time thing. But they were awfully, um, heavy. And if he was that way with her and dropped her immediately afterwards, that says a lot about him, doesn't it?"

So now I knew why Noah didn't like Harris. "You don't think it was a one-time thing, do you?"

He squirmed in his seat. "I was getting Avery's coat for her. I was in the backseat of her car, searching the floor. They didn't see me at first. I overheard Harris tell Gwyn that he loved her. Then they got busted and Harris saw me."

The rational part of my brain said that it was in the past. Homecoming had been almost seven months earlier. But their being together as a secret couple made so much sense. They shared a long history. They may have wanted to keep it secret so that Gwyn's brother wouldn't find out. Harris could have been helping Gwyn this entire time. A memory of running into him at his locker minutes after the office keys were discovered hit me. What if Harris had been out making a copy of the keys and that was why he had rushed to school so late? What if every time he'd said his dad called it had actually been Gwyn? He had canceled dates, left early, made excuses—all for her.

"Are you saying that Harris has been using me this whole time? That the only reason he's been with me is to help his real girlfriend?" I touched the pearl dangling from its chain.

I thought the gift had meant something. Now it felt like a token of betrayal.

"I'm sorry."

My first real boyfriend, I thought. My first romantic moment gazing at the stars had been nothing more than a carefully choreographed scheme, and I had fallen for it. He'd never wanted me. He was going to dump me as soon as Gwyn's problems were fixed and her house felt safe again. All this time, I'd thought Harris was jealous of Noah. He wasn't—he was simply trying to make sure Noah stayed away from me so I wouldn't learn about homecoming.

"Let's go," I said, trying to make myself sound stronger than I felt.

"You sure?"

"Yes. Let's figure this out once and for all."

Noah put the car in Drive and followed the tree-lined street to the cul-de-sac. I saw Mom's car parked in front of the familiar house. Shane's van was behind it.

"Ready?" Noah asked.

I nodded. He put his hand on mine. "If you want, I'll beat the crap out of him later."

That made me smile. "Thanks, Noah, but I think I can handle this one."

"You sure? Because I'm not afraid to hit below the belt if I have to, and let's face it, Harris is a big guy. I may have to."

"No hitting." I squeezed his hand. "But I appreciate the thought."

We got out of the car and approached the house. I didn't bother knocking. I could hear the frantic voices inside, all yelling some strange chant. I opened the door and marched past the foyer and into the living room.

It took me a second to take in everything I was seeing. Beth was there, waving a smoking bunch of sage that filled the room with its sharp, earthy odor. Mom stood near her, reading from her red notebook. A woman I didn't know but figured was Lisa was also reading, her voice louder than the rest. Shane was behind a camera, and finally, off to the side was Gwyn, wrapped tightly in Harris's arms. They were both watching Beth, but Harris was whispering something in her ear and she was nodding.

I wanted to run across the room and pull his arms off her, demand an explanation even though I already knew it and make him beg me for forgiveness. I wanted to tell my mom what Harris had done so she would call off whatever ceremony they were conducting. We could all storm out and tell Gwyn she'd have to live in a creepy house forever and it was all her fault for being manipulative.

They hadn't seen me yet. No one had—they were all too focused on the cleansing ceremony and, it appeared, an up-holstered armchair in the center of the room. As I watched, the chair wobbled slightly and moved across the floor an inch. Then a framed picture hanging on the wall behind me came down with a crash. I jumped, and suddenly everyone was looking at me and Noah.

Mom shot me a quizzical glance but kept on reading aloud from her notebook. I turned my attention to Harris and Gwyn. They both looked back at me with wide eyes. Harris loosened his arms around Gwyn, but only a little. I stayed where I was, debating whether or not I should stomp out of the house or help the team. Beth made the decision for me.

"We need to join hands," she announced. She motioned toward me and Noah. "We could use more help. I'm glad you two are here."

I sighed and joined everyone else as they formed a circle, making sure that I was nowhere near Gwyn or Harris. Noah held my right hand while Lisa grabbed my left. She had the same straight blond hair as Gwyn. Her clammy palm and loud breathing told me how scared she felt. She was also clutching my hand too hard, like she was afraid she might get pulled away at any moment.

Beth lit some candles and closed her eyes. She began singing something in a low voice. Then she asked Lisa to reclaim her home. Lisa clenched my hand again, then spoke in a clear, quivering voice. "This is my home. You have caused us harm. You must leave. You can no longer stay here." The words sounded carefully rehearsed. Lisa repeated them several times, her voice gaining strength each time. Then Beth asked us all to repeat the lines.

"Focus your attention," Beth said. "Take all your fear and anger and channel it into this one purpose."

I had plenty of anger to channel. And while some of the others looked afraid, I was pissed. I thought about Harris while I chanted the lines aloud.

"You have caused us harm." His goal from the second we met was to use me. He sent me roses, gave me jewelry, pretended to be jealous of Noah—and none of it meant anything.

"You must leave." When we had sat in the dark parking lot of the drive-in and he'd told me about Gwyn, he had told half truths. He said their relationship had changed after her brother went to college, and it had: they had gotten closer. And he'd kissed me because he and Gwyn really had gotten into a fight that night. He was mad at her and, once again, using me. When he wasn't manipulating me to help her he was using me to get back at her.

"You can no longer stay here." My reward for helping him was an invitation to prom, an invitation he'd made only after I'd said I would get my parents to look into Gwyn's case. And here I was, wearing my stupid orange prom dress and dirty running shoes while doing exactly what he had wanted me to do all along: help his precious Gwyn.

As we chanted, furniture moved slightly and pictures trembled on the walls. Lisa gripped my left hand so tightly I could barely feel my fingers. Noah was holding on, too, but his grasp was warm and secure. I kept my eyes focused on the chair in the center of the room so I wouldn't have to look at either Harris or Gwyn. I tried to do what Beth asked: channel my feelings and direct it toward our purpose. I wasn't doing it for Gwyn or her mom. I was doing it for my mom, who was obviously working hard to help this family. It was just another case, I told myself. And the Silvers always approached their cases seriously.

We finished chanting and Beth took over again. The room had quieted down, the furniture no longer thumping the floors. I had seen stationary objects do many things, but not all at once and not so continuously. I hated to admit it, but Gwyn had been right: something strange resided in her home.

"Please bring me the box," Beth said.

Gwyn broke the circle and retrieved a cardboard box from the corner of the room. Beth pulled a Ouija board out of it. She set the board on the floor and began taking other objects out of the box, items that supposedly brought people into closer communication with the dead. Beth examined each object before returning everything to the box. Then she placed the box in the living room fireplace and lit the entire thing with her burning sage.

The flames quickly devoured the box and its peculiar contents. As the fire burned, I felt Lisa relax her grip. I tried to understand what had happened in her home. Maybe there had been some strange activity, but my guess was that the family had made the situation even worse. They had unwittingly invited more negative energy into their space each time they'd experimented with different things. The one hundred candles may have contributed to the chaos as much as the Ouija board.

I don't know how long we stood around the fireplace, but after a while I realized the room was dark. Hours had passed since Noah and I had arrived, the sun had set and I was feeling hungry. Finally, Beth announced that we could release hands. "We have restored calm," she said.

"It's done? It's over?" Lisa asked.

"I'd like to bless each room and stay the night to make sure," Beth said. "But, yes, I think we were successful."

I guess we had been expecting a final occurrence, some crazy rush of activity followed by complete silence or a light wind. Instead, the house was perfectly quiet. We all looked around us and then it was like everyone exhaled at once. Shane began clapping, then the rest of us did, too. While Lisa hugged Gwyn and thanked Beth, Mom walked over to me.

"Honey, what are you doing here?"

I shook my head. "It's a long story." I paused. "What was here? Gwyn said it mentioned pushing back the curtain. Was it the Watcher from Ohio?"

"No. I don't think so. Something similar, but not quite as strong."

Harris came up to us, and I realized he had never met my mother. "This is Harris."

"Hello." She looked at him with a confused expression. "I thought you were here with Gwyn."

"He is." My voice came out hard and more than a little bitter.

"Oh. I see."

Harris looked panicked. "Please don't hold it against Gwyn," he said, talking fast. "You won't undo any of this, right? I mean, she's safe now?"

"This is now the safest location in town." Mom turned to me. "I'll give you guys a few minutes. But I'll be home in a little while, okay?"

She walked away without saying anything else to Harris and joined Noah across the room. It was just me and Harris for the moment.

"Don't worry," I told him. "My mother would never undo anything. I don't think she even knows how. Your girlfriend's house is fine."

"I'm sorry, Charlotte, I really am." He shoved his hands in his pockets. "I don't know what to say."

"How long were you planning on stringing me along?" I asked. "If I hadn't been here today, what were you going to do? Dump me tomorrow?"

"No!" He looked at me, taking in my orange dress. "I asked you to prom and I meant it. I was going to take you, honest."

"Right. So a date to prom was my consolation prize." I pulled at the necklace he'd given me until it snapped off. "This is yours. Or Gwyn's. Whatever." I thrust it at him and he took it. "I'd give back the roses, too, but they're dead."

"Um, yeah. About that." He was fixated on the necklace in his hands. "I didn't send those. I don't know who did."

I sighed. "What *did* you do, Harris? And why?"

"We were desperate," he began. "Gwyn needed help, but no one knew what to do. I made copies of the school keys, and we would go in at night." He closed his hand around the necklace. "We ransacked the library, moved chairs. Gwyn sprayed peach air-freshener in the air vents. We used some old video stuff from her attic to make the dog appear. She was the white-haired girl in the video. We needed to get your attention."

"Why? My mom was helping Gwyn's mom. You didn't need me."

Harris sighed. "We didn't know that. Gwyn's mom moved out a few months ago. Gwyn hasn't had a lot of contact with her."

I gave a short, bitter laugh. "So I guess you never really needed me, after all."

"Sorry." It was a whispered apology.

"I have to know," I said, my mind still struggling to assemble all the pieces. "How did you pull off the cell phone thing?"

He looked perplexed. "That wasn't us, I swear."

I could hear Lisa talking to Beth. I looked over at them and locked eyes with Gwyn, who was watching Harris and me from across the room.

"So I guess you two got everything you wanted," I murmured. "And now you can go back to being a happy couple."

"I'm sorry," he said. "I think you're great, I really do. And I like you, but…"

"But you love Gwyn," I finished.

He gave me a helpless look. "Sorry."

I was done with his apologies. "Do me a favor," I said. "Don't talk to me, don't look at me. Stay out of my way and out of sight for the rest of the year, okay?"

He nodded. "Okay." I thought he would put up at least a little resistance, or insist that we be friends. The fact that he didn't made me feel even worse.

I turned my back on him and walked out the door and into the warm night. I made it to the car without crying, but once I got into the passenger seat, it all came out: my anger at

Harris and Gwyn, my disappointment in myself for not seeing what was going on and, finally, the awful and utter pain of my wounded heart.

The driver's-side door opened and Noah slid into his seat. "Let's get you out of here," he said. I nodded and tried to stifle my tears. It was a clear night and I knew that if I craned my neck and looked out the window, I would see a hundred stars.

And that would break my heart even more.

# twenty

He made me tea. As soon as we got back to my house, Noah ordered me to sit on the sofa. Then he brought me a pillow and blankets from the guest room and found the kettle, boiled water and brought me a steaming mug of Calming Chamomile.

"I'm not sick," I protested.

Noah sat next to me on the sofa. "Yeah, I know, but this is what I do for my mom whenever she breaks up with a guy."

"I didn't break up with Harris. He broke up with me." I sipped my drink. I normally didn't like tea, but Noah had added sugar, so it tasted good.

"His loss," Noah said softly.

"You think?" I set down my cup on the coffee table. I knew Harris would have no trouble moving on. He was probably wrapped around Gwyn at that exact moment, telling her how there was no one else in the world for him and reassuring her that we had shared nothing but hollow kisses.

"Hey." Noah cupped my chin in his hand. "I mean it. It's his loss. You are amazing. Truly, completely amazing."

I wanted to believe him, I really did. But if he thought I was so amazing, why had he turned cold at homecoming?

Why couldn't Noah be my first boyfriend? I decided in that moment that I had nothing to lose. If I told him my true feelings and he rejected me, it wouldn't be so bad. It would just be one more bruise to my heart, and maybe I could spend the next few weeks mending my emotions.

"Noah," I began. His hand was still under my chin, holding it up lightly. I looked into his green eyes, and before I could change my mind, I leaned in and kissed him. He was definitely surprised. But he moved his hands to my back and pulled me closer. I had to keep myself from smiling.

He was the first to break our kiss. "Wow. Okay, that was… unexpected."

"Good unexpected or bad unexpected?"

He sat back, but kept one arm around me. "Excellent unexpected," he decided. But he looked worried.

"What is it?" I wasn't sure I wanted to know the answer.

"Was that your way of getting back at Harris?"

"No!" I reached out for his hands. "I mean, yes, I'm upset about Harris, but he made me realize that you're the one I want to be with. I like you. I've always liked you. But after homecoming, you seemed so distant."

"Yeah. I know." He sighed. "You may not remember this, but while we were dancing you started talking about Shane and my mom. I realized that if they broke up, it could be weird for us. Their relationship was so new, and it seemed like the wrong time for us to start something." He offered me a tiny smile. "And I wasn't sure if you liked me as a friend or as something more."

"Let me be clear, then—I like you as something more."

We kissed again, longer this time. He tasted like cinnamon and felt warm. I think I could have stayed there for hours, but the hallway clock chimed eleven.

"It's really late," Noah said. He traced a finger around my top lip.

"Almost the start of a new day," I agreed. "Thank you for making this a really, really good day."

"Let's try to make it a great day," he murmured as he leaned in for another kiss.

I let my fingers get tangled in his hair. I allowed myself to be completely absorbed in the moment, which was a wonderful, crazy moment. I let myself feel...happy.

"Charlotte? Are you here?" It was my dad. He was in the kitchen and must have come through the back door. I snapped back from Noah, reached for my mug of tea and hoped my face wasn't flushed from all the kissing.

"In here, Dad!" I yelled. Noah was busy trying to look like the only thing we'd been doing was discussing politics. He crossed one leg over the other and actually folded his hands in his lap.

"Charlotte!" Dad sounded relieved yet anxious. "I'm so glad I found you. Where's your mother?"

"She's still at Gwyn's—I mean, Lisa's house," I said. "Is everything okay?" Obviously, it was not. My first thought was that something had happened to Annalise.

"Get your stuff," Dad said. He opened the hall closet and grabbed some jackets. "We need to leave."

"Why? Dad, what's going on?" I shared a worried glance with Noah. Dad didn't seem to even register that Noah was there. We heard someone at the back door. Dad froze. Then it opened and Mom came in.

"Why was the back door locked?" she asked.

"Karen." Dad dropped his armful of jackets. "I got a message today. I've been looking for you."

"A message?" Mom had a quizzical smile on her face.

"Zelden's in the hospital. In New Zealand. He was attacked several days ago."

Mom's smile dissolved. "No."

"He was conscious today, and asked one of the hospital staff to call me. He said that the amethyst was broken."

*The amethyst is broken.* Zelden had called me in Charleston and said the same thing. He'd asked me to tell my parents, but I hadn't because it seemed so silly and everyone was getting along so well.

"Charlotte, Noah, let's go. We have to get out of here." Mom had her keys and was walking through the kitchen. "We'll take two cars," she told Dad.

"Will someone please tell me what's going on!" I yelled louder than I should have, but seeing my parents operating in panic mode was freaking me out.

Mom stopped. "Zelden is trying to warn us," she said. "That was our code. *The amethyst is broken* means that Marcus knows where we are and is on his way here." She looked at my dad. "It also means that Zelden's in distress. How long has he been in the hospital?"

I remembered Zelden's voice when he'd called me. Except for a lot of coughing, he'd sounded okay. But if he was trying to pass along a coded message, maybe Marcus had been right there. I could see it: Marcus holding the phone to Zelden's ear, commanding him to speak normally and tell me everything was fine. *It was nice to have met you,* Zelden had said at the end of the call. Why hadn't I realized how final that sounded? Marcus had likely attacked Zelden the moment after he hung up the phone.

"Zelden's been hospitalized for five days now," Dad said grimly.

"That's more than enough time for Marcus to find a way from New Zealand to South Carolina. We'll head to

Charleston, get Annalise and figure out an escape plan on the way. Noah, you're coming with us. We'll have your mom and Shane meet us."

I plucked my purse off the coffee table and retrieved my necklace from inside. My hands were shaking as I tried to clasp the amethyst around my neck. Noah noticed and clasped it for me. As soon as the purple rock touched my skin, something happened. It began to quiver. I curled my hand around it, and the rock buzzed, like I was trying to hold a bee.

"Back door's locked!" Dad hollered. "We're leaving."

As we made our way toward the front door, the lights flickered. Mom stopped, her hand on the doorknob. The lights flickered again and then went out completely. We stood in the dark. I could hear Dad breathing. "I'm getting a flashlight," he said quietly. "Karen, lock the door."

I heard the click of the lock and the sound of Dad rummaging through a kitchen drawer. I was having a hard time adjusting to the blackness. It was too dark, I thought. Usually the streetlights cast a little glow into the house.

"Dining room," Mom whispered. "Now." She held my hand and I held Noah's. My leg bumped into the sofa. I sat down with Noah, but Mom went to the window and pulled back a corner of the curtain.

"The whole street's out," she announced.

Dad came back with the flashlight, but he cupped his hand over it so there wasn't a beam. He stood next to Mom. "What is that?" he whispered. There was fear in his voice. "Is that… is that a dog?"

I had to see. I got up and pushed my way in between Mom and Dad. Our street was cloaked in black, so it was difficult to spot anything. I saw something in the middle of the road, a lumbering dark shape moving slowly. It looked like a large, wounded animal. Something about its staggered movement wasn't right, and its front legs were too long.

I kept staring, trying to make sense of the thing in the road. It lifted its head, sniffed and then turned in our direction. I saw a wide smile spread across its face. I saw the white teeth and the black eyes and I knew that it wasn't an animal crawling on all fours.

It was Marcus.

# twenty-one

There was no time to register the fact that a grown man was crawling across the street and into our front yard. Within seconds, he was pounding on the front door.

"Char—lotte," he sang out in a sickeningly sweet tone. "Time to come out, princess." It was the voice I remembered, the awful blend of male and female and something else. Demon, I guessed. "Be a good girl, Charlotte. Didn't you like my roses?"

I sucked in my breath. Of course. The thirteen roses I had placed on my nightstand, foolishly thinking Harris had sent them.

The Watcher coughed. "I tried calling you, Charlotte."

The cell phones at school. Noah was right—the four digits were a date. It was now past midnight. It was April 13.

"Back door," Mom whispered.

We bolted through the foyer and into the kitchen. But when Dad flung open the door, there was Marcus, leaning against the doorframe and panting. Mom screamed. Dad slammed the door shut and pushed his body against it so he could turn the dead bolt. The door shook as Marcus tried to break it down.

Mom grabbed me by one arm and ran to the living room. Noah was right behind us.

"Here." Mom tossed Noah her car keys. "You two get out of here as soon as you can." She grabbed the iron poker that was propped against the fireplace we never used. "We'll distract him."

"Mom, no!" I was frantic. "We should all go together! I'm not leaving anyone behind!"

She fixed her gaze on Noah. "Get her out of here. No matter what happens, you two need to get out. Find a safe haven. Go to—" Her voice was drowned out by Dad.

"He's almost in!" he yelled from the kitchen.

Mom reached into her pocket and checked her cell phone. Its blue light lit up her face in the dark room. "No service. Call the police when you're away from the house."

"I'm not leaving you!" I screamed.

We heard a loud crack. Dad grunted as the door came down. He staggered into the living room and Mom rushed to his side. "Honey?"

Dad was holding his head. "I'm fine. It's nothing."

Marcus stood in the arched doorway separating the kitchen from the living room, panting heavily. Dad had ushered us as far back as he could, so that our backs were against the computer tables. Mom chanted something, her shaking voice growing louder, until Marcus laughed.

"That one doesn't work on me."

"You are not welcome here!" Dad yelled. "You must leave now!"

"That doesn't work, either." Marcus took a step forward. He seemed to be having trouble with his legs, like he wasn't in complete control of them.

"What are you?" Dad asked. His voice held both awe and revulsion. "Are you a demon?"

Again, Marcus laughed. It was a hideous sound, an inhuman cackle. "No, I am not a demon." He spoke slowly. "I'm something much, much worse."

He smiled. It was unnatural, as if invisible hands were pulling back both sides of his face, stretching the skin past normal limits. His black eyes scanned the four of us before resting on Noah. "I do not know this one," he said. I locked my fingers in Noah's. He gave them a little squeeze.

Marcus looked at us again, but this time he smiled at my dad. "I know this one," he said. "We've met before."

"What?" Dad sounded genuinely mystified.

"I believe you mean, *pardon me?*"

Dad gasped. He had spent years trying to identify the entity that had passed before him in a deserted jail, years examining footage and returning to the site trying to discover what had interacted with him. "It was you?" he whispered.

Marcus bowed slightly. "In the flesh." He cackled at his own little joke. "I have followed you for years. I have been waiting for one of you to push back the curtain too far."

"What do you want from us?" Mom demanded.

"I want her." Marcus pointed a finger at me.

"Never." Mom's voice was stone. There was a certain finality in it that a normal person would never doubt. Unfortunately, Marcus was not a normal person. He wasn't even a person. I saw Dad reach one hand behind his back. Mom slipped the fireplace poker into his hand, then wrapped one arm around me and the other around Noah. My necklace was still buzzing, but now it seemed so loud that I was sure everyone in the room could hear it.

"Get out," Dad said again. "I don't care what you are. You were not invited into our home."

"I do not require an invitation." Marcus stepped forward again, this time leaning heavily on his right leg. "I require punishment. The girl will be punished for what she witnessed. She crossed a line."

"So have you." Dad charged forward, holding the iron poker like it was a baseball bat. He swung hard at Marcus's head, but it wasn't enough. Marcus raised one hand to block the blow. Then he plucked the poker from Dad's hands, pulled back and rammed it against Dad's chest.

The supernatural force of the blow sent Dad flying—literally—into the dining room. His head slammed against the wall with a muffled thump and he landed on the floor like a crumpled piece of paper.

"No!" Mom sprinted across the living room and knelt beside Dad. Noah and I were right behind her. It was awful to watch Mom as she cradled Dad's head and put two fingers to his neck. "There's a pulse," she said, choking back tears.

Marcus shuffled into the room. It looked like he was dragging his body, as if he was trying hard to control it. After a few labored steps, he groaned and swayed to one side. The lights flickered on, but they were dim.

"He's losing strength," Mom whispered. "Noah, get her out of here."

But Noah was standing up, his fists clenched. "Leave them alone." His voice was hoarse and determined.

Marcus took another wobbly step forward. "This is not your concern." His black eyes scanned the room and rested on me. His wide, weird smile emerged again. Noah tackled Marcus from the side, throwing his body at him. And, although Marcus appeared weak, he responded to the attack with only a low grunt and a flick of his hand. Noah was knocked to the floor.

"No!" I wanted to go to him, but Noah was already getting to his feet. Marcus rolled his head from side to side, then leaned against a chair. Deflecting Noah had momentarily drained him again.

"Please," Mom said to Noah. "You have to get Charlotte away from here."

He nodded at her, then grabbed my arm and started guiding me toward the front door. I struggled against him. "I'm not leaving without them!" I shrieked. Marcus turned his head in my direction. I could see his eyes more clearly now, the way the black swallowed up everything else.

"I will find you. No matter where you go, I will find you."

It was difficult to break his vacant stare. Out of the corner of my eye, I saw Mom crawl across the floor. She was reaching for something. I kept my gaze on Marcus, hoping it was enough to distract him. He began to move toward me, but I stayed where I was. Mom stood up, and I saw she had the poker. She used both hands and thrust it forward, spearing Marcus in the back.

He howled. It was a long, painful cry. He staggered to the side, then ripped the iron out of his back and turned on Mom. She backed away, trying to put distance between her and Marcus, but also away from Dad. I wanted to run to her, to seize Marcus by his legs and just pull. He was standing directly over her, the poker grasped in both hands, and was ready to plunge it downward. Mom looked up at him, her eyes wide and desperate, then turned her head and looked at me. As Marcus brought the poker down with his full, awful force, Mom screamed at me.

"Get out of here, Charlotte! Find the safe haven!"

They were the last words my mother spoke to me.

# twenty-two

"We need to go back."

I didn't think Noah had heard me. He was talking on his cell phone while driving us away from my house. "I told you, there was an intruder," he was saying. "He attacked two people. They're hurt. No, I can't stay on the line."

He shut his phone and braced the steering wheel with both hands.

"We need to go back," I repeated.

"The police are on their way. Paramedics, too." He stopped at a red light, looked both ways, then drove straight through. "We can get on the highway and be in Charleston in a couple hours."

"I'm not going to Charleston."

"Charlotte, I know you're in shock, but we need to get as far away as possible."

Of course I was in shock. My brain simply could not process what I had witnessed. Marcus had raised his arms above his head and slammed the iron poker into Mom's head. I heard a crack, followed by Mom's choked gasp. Noah yanked me out the door and down the front steps. He shoved me into the passenger seat of Mom's car and was peeling out of the driveway within seconds.

*Find the safe haven.*

Mom's last words before that evil thing had attacked her. I knew she was telling me where to go, but I couldn't think straight. A safe haven. The police? No, she would have said that. She would have told me exactly where to go, but she was afraid Marcus—the Watcher—would know it.

"Turn around," I told Noah.

"I can't do that." He gripped the steering wheel. "We have to get on the highway."

"No, we don't. We're not leading him to Charleston and Annalise. I know where my mom wanted us to go."

Noah coasted to the shoulder of the road. He looked in his rearview mirror. "Tell me quick."

"She wanted us to find a safe haven. And what's the safest place in town?"

He nodded, screeched back into the road and turned at the next light. I hated myself for doing it, for leaving my parents in a pool of blood on the dining room floor, but it was what they had asked me to do. I had failed them too many times already. I had chosen not to give them a message that may have saved their lives. I didn't tell them about any of Zelden's calls. And now they had paid a price. They had received the ultimate punishment.

They couldn't be dead, I told myself. It wasn't possible. Marcus had no reason to kill them. And Zelden had survived an attack in New Zealand, so wasn't it possible that my parents would survive, too? Dad had a pulse. But Mom...

No one could endure that kind of direct blow to the head. It was too much. The crack I'd heard—it was the worst sound in the world, a thousand times more terrifying than the voice that emanated from Marcus.

I wondered if it could be undone, somehow. Maybe there were rules about this. Maybe an injury brought on by the supernatural could also be cured by the supernatural. We would have to act fast, though.

Noah turned sharply into the familiar driveway. There were no lights on in Gwyn's house, but Shane's van was parked in front so that meant both he and Trisha were still there.

"I'll get out first and make sure he didn't follow us," Noah said. I didn't think Marcus could get very far without a vehicle. Of course, he had been lightning fast when he'd surprised us at the back door, but that had seemed to weaken him. It just hadn't weakened him enough.

Noah came around to the passenger side and helped me out of the car. "I got you," he said. I hadn't been injured, but I felt wobbly, and I leaned against him as we walked up the steps of Gwyn's front porch. He rang the doorbell, then tried the handle. It was locked.

"They have to be here," he muttered. "Please be here."

The door opened and Beth immediately ushered us inside. "Where are your parents?" she asked me, looking stricken. Noah shook his head and Beth locked the door behind us. "Charlotte, your dad called me a little while ago and told me about Marcus. Is everything okay?"

I was hopeful. "A little while ago? When?"

"About an hour."

My optimism deflated. "Oh." Marcus found us before we could leave the house.

"I'm sorry," Beth said.

Trisha came running out of the dark living room and engulfed Noah in a hug.

"Are you okay?" she asked.

He whispered something to her. She pulled back, then came over to me. Without a word, she hugged me, too. Shane enfolded me in his arms, then turned to the group. "I'm going over there," he announced.

"No." Noah shook his head. "I called the police. They're on their way."

"If that thing is still there, I'll deal with it." Shane stepped around us, but Noah grabbed his arm.

"Please," he said. "There's nothing you can do for them, and I think we need you here. It's still after Charlotte."

Shane looked at Noah for a moment, then at me. He nodded.

"Why is it so dark in here?" Noah asked. "Did you lose power, too?"

Beth led us into the kitchen, where several cabinets still lay on the unfinished floor and a dozen white candles had been lined up on the counter. "No. After Patrick called, we turned off the power intentionally," she said. "The Watcher draws its strength from power sources. We're trying to limit that strength so that when he gets here..."

"How do you know he's going to find us?" I asked, my panic rising. Mom had sent us here to be safe. If we weren't safe, what was the point?

"We need him to find you," Beth said. "It's the only way we can end this tonight. You could run, but he'll eventually track you down. At least this way, we can protect you and have a solid chance of destroying it."

"Can you do that?" Noah asked. "Can you really destroy him? Because he's strong." His voice got quieter. He had witnessed the same awful things I had. "Stronger than you might think."

Beth lit another candle. They were the votives, I realized, from the night of Gwyn's party. "I need you to describe him," she said to me. "It will help us to be better prepared."

"He's limping," I began. I wasn't sure what kind of details she wanted, so I rattled off everything that occurred to me. "His eyes are black. Mom stabbed him in the back but it only slowed him down. And he says he's not a demon."

Beth stopped lighting the candles. "What does it claim to be?"

"Something worse." The image of Dad curled up on the

dining room floor flashed across my mind. It was immediately followed by my mother's face, caught in surprise and pain, as the poker slammed into her head, and the cracking sound her skull made, a sound worse than any scream could ever be.

"Hey." Noah enveloped my shoulders in his arms. Part of me wanted to sink into his chest and sob, but that would feel too much like giving in and accepting defeat. If I didn't cry, they were still alive. I would fight for them, even if I wasn't sure how, and I would discover a way to save them. It was not too late. It couldn't be.

Lisa entered the kitchen cradling a large box. "Here it is," she said to Beth. "Everything I could find."

Beth began removing sticks of incense, stones and other New Age paraphernalia. "Good. Do you have the salt?"

"Seriously?" I asked. "You think you can sprinkle some salt and wave some sage and that's going to keep this thing from ripping our heads off?" They didn't understand. We needed weapons. Knives or swords or arrows. Something medieval, maybe, something we could shoot at the Watcher before it stepped foot inside the house.

"It's added protection," Lisa said. "It will help."

"Not against this!" I yelled. "I told you, he's not a demon. He can do whatever he wants." I could see his black eyes and the way Mom's head jerked back when she was hit. "And what he wants is to kill me."

Beth put her hand on mine. "I will not allow that to happen, Charlotte."

"Neither will I." Shane sounded angry and determined. "You said we need extra protection, right? Tell us what to do and we'll do it."

Beth assigned everyone different jobs. Everyone except me.

"I need to you to focus," she said gently as I sat down in a kitchen chair and she knelt in front of me. "I want you to picture something good in your mind, a happy moment."

My first thought was the family dinner we'd shared in Charleston on our last night of vacation, the way Mom and Dad had clinked their wineglasses together. The image was immediately replaced with one of Mom and Dad lying on the blood-soaked carpet.

"You can still save them, right?" I asked Beth. She said nothing, but her eyes glistened with tears. Lisa walked in and began gathering more sage from the box. "You've read all the books," I said to Lisa, my voice desperate. "You can help me. There's got to be something that can undo all of this."

Lisa looked to Beth, then back at me. "I'm sorry. I can help protect you, but that's all. Nothing can erase—" She stopped, unwilling to say the word.

Beth stood up. "We will do what we can."

"If we destroy the Watcher, if we send it back to wherever it came from, things will return to normal," I said loudly. "I know it."

I didn't know it, but it was all I had, the only thing I could cling to so I wouldn't fall into absolute despair. Beth and Lisa left the room. I stayed in the kitchen chair, gazing across the room. The foyer separated the kitchen from the living room, but the wide, arched doorways allowed me to see directly into both spaces. Harris was pouring a circle of salt on the living room floor while Noah pushed back furniture. Lisa talked softly to Beth in the foyer, sharing her worries about letting something evil back into the house and where they should send "the kids." Beth said it was too late to leave, but suggested they use the attic. "I just blessed it," she said. "They'll be fine there."

I looked around the kitchen for a working clock, but without power the LED numbers that were usually displayed on a stove or microwave weren't there. I was looking up, hoping to spot a battery-operated clock on the wall, when Gwyn entered the room and I sat up, startled.

"Sorry," she said. "I'm supposed to finish lighting these."

She motioned to the candles on the counter. "I can do it in another room, though."

"No, that's okay." I didn't hate Gwyn. I didn't feel anything for her or Harris. Their actions were insignificant now, and seemed to have happened in another lifetime.

"Beth called your sister," Gwyn said. "I thought you should know. She's driving up with her boyfriend."

"Is there news about my parents?"

"Not that I know of. I called Avery a few minutes ago. She said she'd call me back if she heard anything." She pulled her phone from her pocket and placed it on the counter.

"Thanks." Avery had undoubtedly heard the sirens and seen the flashing police lights. She had probably worried, so it was good that Gwyn had called her, even if the news wasn't positive.

"Charlotte, I am truly sorry. For everything. I know that doesn't make it better." Gwyn finished with the candles and carried some into the living room. While she was gone, her cell phone buzzed. I picked it up and saw that Avery was calling.

"Your dad is at the hospital," she informed me.

"He's alive?" I whispered.

"Yes. I'm going over there with my mom and Jared right now." She was using her panic-mode voice, the tough, take-charge tone she got when there was a problem she was solving.

"And my mom?" I knew the answer, but I was hoping that there was some small, miraculous chance that I was wrong.

"I don't know. I haven't seen her and no one will tell me anything." I heard the jingle of Avery's car keys. "The police haven't found the guy who did this. They've brought in dogs, but something's wrong. The dogs are acting all weird."

That's because the dogs had been trained to track people, not demon-like entities, I wanted to say. I didn't know how much Avery knew or how much time I had to tell her. All

I knew was that I wanted her away from my house and our neighborhood. I needed to know that she was safe. If the Watcher was still nearby, he could take her as a hostage to use against me. I would not allow someone else to be hurt because of me. So much of what had happened in the past hour was my fault. If I had relayed Zelden's message to my parents when we were in Charleston, none of this would be happening. I could feel the guilt burning inside of me, but I pushed it away. For now.

"Go to the hospital," I said. "I'll be there as soon as I can."

"We're thinking about you, Charlotte. Drive safe."

I closed the phone, but not before checking the time. It was almost two in the morning. The glow of candlelight filled the living room, casting bobbing shadows on the walls. I waited for someone to tell me what I needed to do. I thought about my dad and how he was lying in the back of an ambulance at that moment, fighting to survive. I thought about Mom and tried to focus on her smile instead of her body being zipped into a heavy black bag. And then I thought about how I had to face the Watcher now or risk running from it forever.

"Charlotte, we need you in the circle," Beth called. "It's time."

Outside, something howled, low and strong, and a dark shape passed by the window. My necklace buzzed and my heart raced and I knew he had found me. A second later, the front door came crashing across the foyer.

I stood up. The Watcher wanted to punish me, and he had.

Now it was my turn.

# twenty-three

It didn't see me at first. The Watcher dragged itself into the foyer, stumbling over the broken door. It saw the flickering candles, and turned for the living room, where everyone had gathered within the circle of salt. I was still in the kitchen, one foot frozen in the foyer. The Watcher's back was to me, and I could see the jagged line of blood seeping through his shirt where Mom had stabbed its borrowed body. His shoulders were slumped, and his panting breath was the only noise in the room. The trip from my house to Gwyn's must have sapped some of his energy. Hopefully the lack of electricity in the house would drain him even more.

Beth stood tall in front of everyone. Shane, Trisha, Noah and Lisa were behind her, surrounded by the white candles. I didn't see Harris and Gwyn and figured that Lisa had sent them away, into the attic with strict instructions not to come downstairs.

The Watcher stopped a few feet in front of the circle of salt. It was a protected space, one that I should have been standing inside, but I felt better knowing that the people who mattered were there without me. There was less chance of anyone being hurt.

Beth began chanting something, but the Watcher laughed at her, a high-pitched, snarling noise that made me clench my fists with rage. "Those words hold no power over me." His head moved from side to side. "Where is the girl?" he demanded.

I had a choice. I could run through the gaping hole where the front door had been and hope the others could slow the Watcher down. Or I could confront him and pray that when he was done with me it would finally be over, the monster would return to its lair and we would be left with some way to help my parents. I stepped forward.

"I'm right here." My voice wasn't as strong as I had hoped it would be. My necklace buzzed, and I closed my hand around it.

The Watcher turned slowly. He was weaker than he had been at my house, more sluggish. "Char—lotte." He dragged my name out as if he was drunk, a gleeful smile on his dirty face. He barely resembled Marcus anymore. He looked centuries older, his skin wrinkled like old parchment.

Behind him, Beth instructed the others to think only positive thoughts. I knew I should be doing the same thing, but I didn't have the mental strength. I wouldn't be able to fight this thing with love or positive feelings. I had to rely on something else entirely.

It's all about energy. My dad always said that. Positive, negative, good, bad. It was all just energy. As I stared into the black eyes of the Watcher, my hand clutching the amethyst around my neck, I knew we were locked in a battle of his energy versus mine. And what was my energy? What could I possibly possess that was more powerful than the thing making its way toward me?

I held my necklace even tighter, so tight that the jagged ends of the amethyst cut into the palm of my hand. I had seventeen years of life behind me. I had memories and experiences and successes and failures. I knew things. I knew that people could obsess about a person or a place so much that that person left something of themselves behind after they died. I knew that if you focused hard enough and long enough, you could tattoo a piece of your presence somewhere.

So that's what I did. I focused as hard as I could on what I wanted. I wanted my friends and my family to be safe. I wanted the Watcher to go back to the horrible place it had emerged from. I wanted to defeat it, to destroy it, to show it that it had no power over me or my family.

I began chanting my own words. They weren't Latin or Sanskrit or anything mystical. They were simply mine, in the purest form I could think of. My energy, funneled through my voice.

"You have already punished me," I said. "You have shown me what I should not have seen."

The grisly attack on my parents. No one should have to witness that.

"Your goal has been reached, and now you must go back."

"I will never go back," it hissed. The Watcher still struggled with his legs. He reached down with both arms to move them. I knew that even though his movement was limited, his physical strength might still be intact. I didn't want to risk charging into him, only to be tossed across the room like a stone.

My hand hurt. Warm blood trickled from my palm down my arm, but still, I clutched the stone. It vibrated in my hand, and I felt like that gave me vigor, somehow, a little life to carry on.

"You have no right to be here," I continued. "You have

already punished me. There is nothing for you here. You must return."

The Watcher groaned. I looked at him, hunched over only a few feet away from me. I saw Shane in the living room, his eyes wild as he debated running to my rescue. Then Noah broke the circle and ran for it. Trisha screamed, and the Watcher turned around, put out one hand and caught Noah by the neck. He lifted him off the ground effortlessly. "Interesting," he growled, cocking his head to one side. Noah's legs flailed, and he put his hands on the Watcher's, trying to break the hold.

Shane dashed for the Watcher. "Let him go!" he yelled.

The Watcher held out his other arm, but Shane went right for Noah, threw both arms around his torso and pulled. It was an action the Watcher wasn't anticipating. He flinched, and both Noah and Shane tumbled to the floor. Shane hauled a coughing Noah back to the circle, where Trisha held her son. Then Shane stood up and looked right at me.

I had never seen fear written on his face like that. I knew what he wanted to do, and I knew what would happen if he did. "Stay in the circle," I pleaded. Beth spoke softly to him, but I knew I had mere seconds before Shane attempted to help me. If he did, his fate would match my father's. "No," I mouthed. The Watcher had turned around and was looking in my direction again.

The group continued to murmur things, words I suspected were descriptions of their happy memories, an outpouring of positive thinking in the wake of a negative being. Maybe it was having an effect. The Watcher was definitely having trouble, his panting more pronounced, his movements more labored. I felt a surge of hope—I could do this. I could win this battle.

"You pushed back the curtain too far," it gasped.

"That was never my intention." If I stretched my arm, I was sure I could touch his forehead. I held my ground, even though my every instinct was screaming at me to step back.

Instead, I looked into those black eyes one more time. Even in the dim candlelight, I could see something was different. There was a speck of soft white at the edges, a piece of the human Marcus trying to get through. It was still his body—and he was fighting for it.

My hand hurt, but still I squeezed. The buzzing of the amethyst had become a steady pulse, following the same rhythm as my beating heart. I knew then what I had to do. I concentrated on that rhythm, on the blood seeping over the stone. The Watcher took another wobbly step toward me.

"You have seen too much," it wheezed.

I thought of the blood smeared across my living room. "You're right," I said. "I have. And you have taken too much."

I yanked the necklace off and pushed the bloody stone as hard as I could into the Watcher's chest. I pressed it into his ripped shirt, twisting my hand and grinding it into his flesh. He howled in agony, a sound that was half human and half beast and totally deafening. His hands thrashed toward me. I felt sharp fingernails slice through my arm, and even though it stung more than it should have, even though it felt like a hot knife had carved through my skin, I held on to that stone and kept forcing it into the Watcher's chest, as close to his heart as I could get it.

I knew that, for all my skepticism, the amethyst had absorbed something of my energy. I thought of Dad's theories, all of which involved someone leaving a part of themselves behind through sheer, desperate concentration. Inmates in solitary confinement left behind traces of their presence in ancient cells. Distressed widows left behind the sound of their pacing footsteps as they waited for dead husbands to return. And I had poured my worries and thoughts and reflections into the purple stone that had dangled from my neck for months. It had to be enough, I thought. The rock mixed with my blood, my life's energy, had to create something more powerful than this stricken monster could handle.

The Watcher fell to his knees. Shane darted across the room and stood behind me, ready to pull me away. I continued to press the amethyst into the Watcher's chest. He groaned and hissed and made deep, guttural sounds. My own legs were shaking with fear, but Shane was right there, ready to catch me if I fell.

"Punish," the Watcher hissed. His black eyes were fading to gray. It was working. As the Watcher continued to thrash and howl at me, I heard another voice, smaller and more difficult to perceive.

"I tried to stop it." It was a pitiful cry nearly buried beneath the Watcher's voice, but coming from the same body. Marcus was trying to reclaim himself. The gray eyes began to turn white, and I knew the battle was almost over.

Finally, with one last wail, the body fell back. I was left there with the stone in my hand, my head swimming with dizzy exhaustion. I collapsed, too—into Shane's arms, where I closed my eyes and slipped into unconsciousness.

# twenty-four

I didn't notice the blood on my hospital gown until Annalise pointed it out.

"What's that?" she asked.

I looked down at the small stain located on the arm of my faded blue gown. "They had trouble with the IV," I explained.

I remembered a nurse from the night before. "Little pinch," she said as she jammed the needle into my vein. It was not a "little pinch." She should have warned me better. She should have said, "Get ready for a searing pain that will echo throughout your poor arm." Although, after the pain of the previous day, what was a sterilized needle through my arm? It was hardly anything compared to the stitches sewn into the palm of my hand where the amethyst had cut too deeply. And it was nothing when I thought of the pain both my parents had endured.

Annalise poured herself a cup of water from the plastic pitcher by my bedside. She took a sip, then grimaced. "It tastes like chemicals."

"I know. I've been drinking soda."

Annalise was not in my hospital room to drink water and hang out. She needed to tell me something but was trying to work her way up to it. I knew my sister: the longer she waited, the worse the news. I wasn't too worried, though. Both our parents had survived and were recovering in rooms across the hospital.

After the confrontation with Marcus, I had awoken in the hospital with a hazy recollection of people pointing lights in my eyes and poking my veins with IV needles, urging me to wake up. I was also aware of not wanting to wake up, of needing to curl into the warm, safe darkness for as long as possible.

The same doctor who had removed my arm sling months earlier was peering down at me the next morning. "Good," she'd said. "You're awake. You have quite a few people waiting to see you."

Annalise had rushed in and immediately hugged me. "Thank God you're okay," she'd gushed. "The doctor says it's just shock, plus the gash in your hand. And dehydration, for some reason. They're going to keep you overnight for observation."

During my first day in the hospital I did nothing except sleep and answer other people's questions. I talked with so many police officers that their faces blurred together, but there was one who seemed kinder than the rest, an older man who resembled pictures I had seen of my great-grandfather.

"Can you tell us what you remember?" he asked. He was there with a younger officer, a guy who stood off to the side, taking notes.

"We were attacked." I had no idea how much they already knew, so I kept my answers simple.

"Did you know the man who attacked you?" the officer asked gently.

"Is he in jail?"

The younger officer scoffed. "The morgue is more like it."

The older cop shot him a warning glance and then turned back to me. "He died from his injuries."

"Injuries?" I had been the last person to touch Marcus. Had I killed him? Did they think I was a murderer?

After the police left, Annalise filled me in. She said that Beth and Lisa had wasted no time contacting the authorities after the final confrontation with Marcus. It was Beth who'd concocted a credible story. She'd said that Marcus was a disturbed fan. He'd attacked my parents, but Noah and I had escaped and driven to Gwyn's house because we knew that's where Trisha was. Marcus had followed us somehow and attacked again before collapsing. When the police arrived, Beth had cleared the room of all the candles and anything else that might look weird. They were just hanging out, she said, when all hell broke loose.

And now it was over. Shane had brought me a homemade omelet for breakfast, wrapped tightly in tinfoil so it wouldn't get too cold. He and Annalise were taking turns visiting my parents. I was eager to get out of my hospital room and see them for myself.

Annalise turned on the TV mounted to the wall. "There's only five channels," I warned her. "And one is all about recovering from childbirth."

Annalise left the TV on the twenty-four-hour news station, but put it on mute. "They're going to discharge you tomorrow," she said.

"Good. I know it's only been a day, but I'm sick of this bed." I tried to adjust it using the control, but my biggest problem was the flat, papery pillows. I was using four of them and still felt like my head was resting against a pancake.

A nurse entered the room. "Time for vitals!" she sang out.

I actually liked this nurse, if only because she didn't poke me with anything sharp. I automatically held out my arm so she could wrap the blood-pressure cuff over it. Then she took my temperature through my ear, marked some things on my chart and left.

I watched my sister, whose focus was on the silent TV. "I'm waiting, you know."

She didn't look at me. "I know. I'm not ready to tell you yet."

"It's that bad?"

"It's Mom."

I struggled to sit up. "You said she was okay."

"I said she was alive."

My sister looked down at her hands. When she looked up, her eyes were red and shiny with tears. "Charlotte, it's bad. Really bad."

Annalise explained that the doctors had put Mom into a coma. There was swelling in her brain, and no one knew if she would be able to recover completely.

"They were amazed that she even survived," my sister said. "She's in critical condition. We can't do anything now except wait."

I had witnessed the attack. I knew how bad it was. Still, I had held on to a string of hope. Miracles happened. People recovered from awful accidents all the time. Maybe she would shock the doctors and open her eyes and everything would be fine.

"Does Dad know?"

"Shane is telling him now."

I had questions but wasn't sure I wanted to know the answers. We were quiet for a while, each of us staring at the TV and lost in our own thoughts. Then a familiar face flashed across the screen, and Annalise immediately turned on the volume. A brunette news anchor was narrating the hour's top stories.

"Bestselling author and renowned psychic Leonard Zelden was released from a New Zealand hospital today," she reported. "Zelden was attacked by an unknown assailant over a week ago and suffered extensive injuries." The TV showed Zelden being pushed in a wheelchair. Around him, cameras flashed and reporters shouted questions.

"I am so very grateful to the doctors and staff here," Zelden said. He looked frail, and his voice was soft. "I would like to thank my dear fans for their kind support and I look forward to recovering at home."

"Did you have a near-death experience? Will you be writing about it?" someone shouted.

Zelden raised his head and looked directly at the camera. "I have no memory of the attack and do not wish to discuss it further. I will not be writing a book about the experience."

"Thank God," Annalise murmured.

It was a sliver of good news that Zelden would not exploit our trauma for his personal gain. Of course, he had gone through something awful, as well. I wondered how he would handle the aftermath of Marcus's death, or if he even knew about it yet.

There was a light knock at the door. "Hello?" Beth came into the room holding a flower arrangement. White roses and daisies peeked out of a glass vase.

"These are lovely," I said. "Thank you, Beth."

"I wish I could take credit for them, but they're actually from Noah." She set the vase down next to my bed. "He's downstairs. I wanted to speak with you before he came up, if that's all right."

"I'm going to check on Dad," Annalise announced. She turned off the TV. "I'll be back later."

After my sister left, Beth pulled a chair next to my bed. She looked at my bandaged hand. "I would imagine that receiving a dozen stitches in your palm is more than a little uncomfortable."

"You could say that." The doctors had used tweezers to pluck a shard of stone embedded in my hand. I would have scars, but they assured me it wouldn't be so bad, that they would blend in with the natural lines of my palm. I didn't want to think about it. My minor injury could not compare to what had happened to my mother. What if she didn't wake up? Or worse, if she did wake up but was brain damaged?

"Charlotte, I'm sure you have a lot of questions."

I did, but only one seemed to matter at that moment. "Did I destroy it?" I asked. "Is the Watcher gone?"

Beth hesitated. "For the time being, yes. But I don't know if he will return."

It was not the answer I wanted. "So Marcus died and Dad was hurt and my mom might never wake up and for what? For us to have to wait in fear, wondering if that thing is going to hunt us down in the middle of the night?"

Beth accepted my angry outburst with a sympathetic nod. "I don't know. But I do know that it took years for the Watcher to find a suitable host."

"What was it about Marcus? Why did the Watcher pick him?"

"There were probably many reasons." She sat back in her chair. "Marcus may have been an easy target, someone who was susceptible to control. He was near your family at the same time the Watcher was present."

I thought about that cold Christmas morning. My family had had no idea that by entering the sanitarium we were walking into the lair of something that had been waiting for years to hurt us.

"I still don't understand what I did that was so wrong. Why did this thing target us?"

"You did nothing wrong, Charlotte." Beth took my good

hand in hers. "Listen to me. It wasn't you. There are things in this world…" She shook her head. "You have no idea."

"Then give me an idea." I felt the hot sting of tears. "What was it?"

"There are souls that cannot cross. Ever. They lived terrible lives and now they are trapped. It's their punishment. They cannot move on, but they cannot go back. So they look for ways to enter this world."

"And this particular soul entered through Marcus."

"Yes. And he—it—holds an awful rage toward anyone who can cross over, even if only for a moment. The Watcher wants to hurt those who are not imprisoned the way it is."

"So it's a revenge thing." I leaned back on my flat pillows. "Is there more than one? Gwyn heard the same voice I did, but Mom said it wasn't the same thing."

"There is more than one. More than a hundred, more than a thousand. But the one that came after you was particularly old and powerful."

"And could return again."

Beth squeezed my hand. "We'll be ready. I promise you that."

She stood up. "Noah is waiting, so I'll go."

"Thanks for coming to see me."

She patted my leg. "Of course. And Charlotte, I'm praying for your mother. She is a good friend and a wonderful person. I believe she will recover."

I wished that I could share that belief, but I wasn't as confident. The only thing that cheered me up even a little was Noah's arrival, but even that was dulled when I saw what had happened to him. Five bruises formed a dark ring beneath his jaw. It was the mark left by the Watcher when he had lifted Noah by his neck.

"Do you like the flowers?" he asked.

"Yes." I couldn't stop staring at the deep black bruises. They covered most of his neck, and at first glance, they resembled a strange tattoo.

Noah sat on the edge of my bed. He picked up my bandaged hand and held it. "I'm sorry," he whispered. "I'm sorry I couldn't do anything to stop it."

"There was nothing you could do." I was shocked that he felt any guilt. He had been dragged into a horrible situation because of me. If he hadn't been in my house when it had all begun, he would be fine.

Not knowing what I could say to make things right, I leaned forward and softly kissed his cheek. He bowed his head so that our foreheads were touching, and we sat that way, with our eyes open, for a long time.

I spent the next night sleeping in a chair by Dad's bedside. He looked terrible, with his head bound in gauze and his arm propped up in a thick white cast. It was his eyes that bothered me most, though. There was nothing but numb grief in them. He tried to smile at Annalise and me when we visited, and we tried to smile back, but it was hopeless.

The following morning, after Annalise had left the room to get coffee from the cafeteria, Dad broke down sobbing. I knelt on the floor, took his pale hand in mine and confessed everything. I told him about Gwyn's party and Zelden's calls and the thirteen roses. I begged him to forgive me for not telling him about Zelden's final message, the code that could have saved Mom. When I was done, he reached down and put his one good hand on my cheek.

"This was not your fault, Charlotte." He sounded hoarse. "If I hadn't allowed things to get so tense between your mother and me, if I had only listened to her in the first place, we wouldn't be here right now."

"No," I said. "It's not your fault, either. Please don't think it is, Dad." I hugged him, and we cried some more.

"Have you been to see her yet?" Dad asked.

I shook my head. "No." While part of me was desperate to visit her, another part was terrified to see her hooked up to wires and beeping monitors. I didn't know if I was strong enough to handle it.

"Make sure you do," Dad said. "Make sure she hears your voice. She needs to know that you're okay."

With her injuries, I doubted my mother would even be aware of my presence, but I promised my dad I would talk to her. Annalise returned with two cups of steaming coffee. She handed one to my dad, and the three of us spent some more time together. When Dad fell asleep, I decided to keep my promise to him.

"Do you want me to go with you?" Annalise whispered. She pulled a blanket around Dad.

"I think I want to go alone." We went out into the hallway. "Maybe you could walk with me to her room, though?"

Annalise hugged me. "Absolutely. This way."

We took an elevator to the intensive care unit. It was a loud floor, filled with the busy rush of nurses and the constant noise of different monitors. Mom's room was near the end of the hallway. We checked in at the nurse's station. Annalise waited there while I walked past the closed doors of the other rooms, trying not to imagine how many people had died behind them. When I got to Mom's room, I stopped for a moment, my bandaged hand on the door. I could hear the heart monitor inside, and the heavy whooshing of a ventilator. I looked back at my sister, who simply nodded. I took a deep breath.

Then I opened the door.

# twenty-five

We sat on the front porch of Avery's house, listening to a thousand unseen crickets fill the warm night with their rhythmic chattering. I rested against Noah, careful not to get too close to his neck. It was difficult to look at him and not immediately see the bruises. Sitting next to him made it easier.

"When do you think they'll leave?" I asked.

We watched the lights up the hill, the ones that flooded the entire downstairs of my house. White vans cluttered the driveway. Every few minutes, someone would exit the house and slide open a van door to put something in or take more equipment out.

"Should be soon," Noah said. "They've been there for hours now."

The front door opened and Avery joined us on the steps. "They're still working?"

"Yes. I want to stay out here until they leave, if that's okay."

"Stay as long as you like. We're roommates, so this is your house, too." She slipped off her shoes and let her bare feet rest in the grass.

"You guys don't need to sit with me," I said. "I know it's depressing."

Noah kissed the top of my head. "I'm not going anywhere."

"Me, neither," Avery said. "Besides, there are too many people inside right now."

Shane and Trisha were cleaning up the dinner dishes. They had ordered Avery's mom out of the kitchen, insisting she had done more than enough for one day. And she had. It wasn't simply that she had hosted dinner for all of us, which included Annalise, Mills, Beth and Jared. She had taken care of so many details over the past week, things that never would have occurred to me. She was the one who contacted professional cleaners to go into my house, the same cleaners we were now watching from Avery's front porch.

They had their work cut out for them.

Since being released from the hospital, I had been inside my house only one time. Beth went with me so we could pack an overnight bag for Dad, but she understood that I needed a moment by myself, in the room where everything had happened. So while she was upstairs going through the closet, I had a chance to confront the aftermath of that night. I stood in the foyer, which was still cordoned off with limp yellow police tape, and wondered why the police and paramedics didn't clean up after themselves. That was my initial thought after seeing my house for the first time: what a mess.

I put my hand on the tape, wondering if it was illegal to rip it down. Was it still considered a crime scene? But, no, the officer I had spoken with that morning said I had permission to be there. I had never before needed authorization to enter my own home, but now I could see why they had kept me away.

I stepped under the police tape, unwilling to be the one

responsible for tearing it down, and surveyed the dining room. The sofa remained where it had always been, but the coffee table had been pushed against a wall and a lamp was tipped over. It wasn't so bad, I thought.

Then I looked down. My eyes followed a path of muddy footprints to the corner of the room where Dad had fallen. Smeared on the pale wall was a single bloody handprint.

Dad had regained consciousness before the paramedics had arrived. He had seen my mother, and tried to stand up and walk to her. He hadn't had the strength, though, and had ended up crawling across the carpet, leaving a trail of dark blood. The police had found him cradling her motionless body. I'd overheard a nurse describe how the paramedics had to pry him off her, that he'd refused to let go.

The trail of Dad's blood ended across the room. A larger stain marked the spot where Mom had been hit, and all around it were strips of gauze and plastic casings the paramedics had ripped open and discarded. I could only stare at the scene, unable to grasp that everything had really happened right here, in my house.

I thought about that as I sat on Avery's porch and saw a man exiting my house with a long roll of carpet balanced on his shoulder. He tossed the carpet into a van and removed a newer roll, still wrapped in plastic. I took it to mean that they had finished painting over the bloody walls and were moving on to installing the new flooring.

"Making progress," I murmured.

I only wished my mother could make progress of her own. My visit to her hospital room had been brief. I was over-whelmed by the sight of her, sleeping and still, with her head heavily bandaged. Clear tubes connected her pale arms to different machines. She did not look like herself, I thought, but more like a wax figure.

A nurse had entered the room. She gave me a brisk nod and checked Mom's chart, adjusted the IV and quietly left. I stood at the foot of Mom's bed, desperately trying to think of something to say to her.

I managed to choke out two words before fleeing the room. "Love you."

I had spent the past three nights in Avery's room. Her mother tended to me as if I was a wounded animal, bringing me lentil soup and constantly covering me with blankets.

The front door of Avery's house opened again. Annalise poked her head out. "Dad called—he wants to talk to you," she said. I got up and took the phone from her. "Hey, Dad."

"Charlotte! Good news. I'm being released tomorrow."

"That's great." His voice didn't sound as hoarse as it had a few days earlier, but his enthusiasm was definitely forced. I knew he was trying to stay positive for us. I also knew it couldn't last.

"I'll be staying with Shane for a while," he continued. "Do you think Avery will mind having you for another week?"

"Not at all." I waited for him to mention Mom, but I already knew from my sister that there had been no change in her condition.

"I'll see you tomorrow, okay?"

"Okay, Dad. Love you."

"Love you, too."

I returned to the porch. One of the vans was gone, and it looked like the cleaners were loading the other vans with their stuff. "Are they done?" I asked.

"I think so," said Avery.

We watched as the rest of the vans pulled away. My house was dark except for the porch light. I wanted to walk up the hill. I wanted to step into my house and smell new carpet and fresh paint instead of the iron tang of old blood.

Beth put her arms on my shoulders and I jumped. "I didn't realize you were out here," I mumbled.

"Are you ready?" she asked.

"Ready for what?"

She walked down the porch steps. "It's time to help your mother."

We sat in a small circle, a hundred unlit candles in front of us. They were the same kind of white votives we had used at Gwyn's, only these were brand new. I looked at the people sitting with me. Shane and Trisha were across the circle, along with Annalise and Mills. Jared, Avery and Noah were there, too. Beth held a box of matches in her hand as she addressed us.

"This is not a game. It is a sacred ceremony, one that was created to help the living grieve for their dead." She picked up a candle. "It is also a way to reach out to those who are suffering and need strength."

At first, I had resisted the idea of returning to my house with everyone. But Beth explained that it was necessary to reclaim the space, to bless it in order to diminish some of the horror that had occurred there. And she believed the best way to do that was to surround ourselves with people who knew and loved Mom.

It was good to see the dining room back to a more normal state. The new paint was a shade darker, the carpet a little softer. Beth was careful to arrange us so that none of us were sitting in the exact spots where the heaviest bloodstains had been. Instead, we occupied the middle of the room.

"After you describe a memory of Karen Silver, you will light one of the candles," Beth said. "It should be a good memory, something that happened with her. After all the candles have been lit, we will send her our good wishes and prayers for her recovery."

I remembered the original one hundred candles, and how the night had dragged on as people had searched for stories. I knew it would not be as difficult to conjure one hundred memories of my mother. We could light a thousand candles and it would not be enough.

Jared went first, which surprised me. He'd only met my mother a couple times that I knew of. "I came to see Mrs. Silver a few months ago," he said. "I asked her for advice on what I could do for Adam. The memorial was her idea."

I listened to the others tell some of their stories first. I loved hearing about the different ways she'd helped people or made them laugh or simply maintained a kind and supportive nature. I could picture her clearly when Shane described an outing to an old school where the sound of children laughing had been reported. When Mom heard an unmistakable giggling coming from behind her, she turned around and laughed along with the energy, and when Shane said the sound gave him the creeps, Mom tickled him until he laughed, too.

Half the candles had been lit by the time I found my voice and chose a story I wanted to tell.

"When I was seven I decided it was time for me to accompany my family on a night investigation." I explained that up until that point, I'd only gone with them during the daytime. My dad wasn't sure that I was ready to handle a trip at night, even though he was the one who always pointed out that if a place was supposedly haunted at night, then it was just as haunted in the daytime. Still, he didn't want me to get scared at such a young age. He thought one bad experience would scar me for life. Mom disagreed. She said it was my choice, and if I wanted to go, I could.

We pulled up to a Victorian mansion just as the sun was

setting. I bounded out of the van, ready to prove myself. But as soon as I walked inside the cavernous house, my bravery crumbled. I wanted to hide in the van with the doors locked and never come out. Before I could confess my fears, Mom pulled me aside.

"I know it's dark in here," she said. Her soft voice echoed off the dusty walls. "But always remember this—we're all here together, even in the dark, even when you can't see us."

She held my hand for a long time. When I was finally ready to let go, it was only because I knew she was still there, even if I couldn't see her.

I lit my candle and nudged it toward the others. Before long, all one hundred were lit. The dining room filled with the warm light of the flickering votives. I closed my eyes, willing myself to stay strong for her sake. I knew the days and weeks in front of me would be filled with waiting. My world would never return to the normal I once knew.

I reached for the necklace I had grown so familiar with wearing and, once again, realized it was not there. Beth would give me a new one if I asked. I wondered if there was a stone for hope. And I wondered, as I opened my eyes and looked around at everyone in the room, if I even needed to depend upon a small rock when I was lucky enough to have strong friends instead.

★ ★ ★ ★ ★

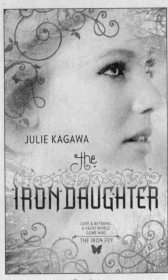

JULIE KAGAWA

the

IRON QUEEN

SUMMER FADES.
ICE MELTS.
HERE'S WHAT'S LEFT.
THE IRON FEY

## Available Now

Half-faery princess Meghan has been banished to
the human world, along with her love, Winter faery prince Ash.
But when a new Iron King rises to make war on all of Faery,
they must return to save the world they both love...
even if it means losing each other forever.

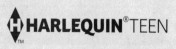

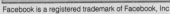
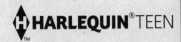